About th

Now enjoying retirement, Hettie lives in Buckinghamshire with her husband and two cats. Much of her time is devoted to her related passions of sewing, quilting and social history.

In her working years she developed an interest in the barriers women faced in all aspects of life, particularly relating to health, family and work.

She has been heartened to witness, in recent decades, the widening of opportunities for women, although the life/work balance continues to be tricky for most.

In her own career Hettie helped to support families as a nurse, midwife and health visitor.

Writing this, her first book has been an enjoyable and challenging experience.

THREADS OF STEEL

Hettie Aston

THREADS OF STEEL

Vanguard Press

A CIP catalogue record for this title is
available from the British Library.

ISBN 9781784657 49-9

*Vanguard Press is an imprint of
Pegasus Elliot MacKenzie Publishers Ltd.*
www.pegasuspublishers.com

First Published in 2020

**Vanguard Press
Sheraton House Castle Park
Cambridge England**

Printed & Bound in Great Britain

Dedication

To Brenda, a friend much missed.

CHAPTER ONE

September 1931

It was early September 1931 and I realised for the first time that it is possible to be both torn apart by grief and, at the same time, filled with the fury of an Erinyes.

I was fifteen years old as I walked slowly behind the hand cart which carried my mother's simple, plain wooden coffin. Her boss Jim and his mate Harry pushed the cart — it wasn't heavy.

Nearly everyone from our village of Little Laxlet was there, as well as the people from the farms and the hamlets round about. There was no birdsong. The sound of our feet trudging slowly towards the Chapel was the only sound. A heavy, grey sky signalled an impending storm and the air felt thick with sadness.

Herbert Flitch, my Stepfather, looking ridiculous in his top hat, head bowed and very much acting the grieving widower, was first behind the cart. His mother, dressed in black funeral clothes, including a long black face veil, walked beside him. The baby, in the arms of Mrs Flitch, was wrapped in a beautiful fine woollen Shetland shawl, lovingly knitted by my mother during her pregnancy.

The cold, austere Chapel wasn't too far from our cottage and the minister was waiting for us by the big, oak front door. He nodded in solemn greeting as we arrived, as only men of the cloth can, and I remember thinking in that moment, 'Nodding must be part of their training at Minister's college.'

As we followed him inside there was a huge flash of lightening followed quickly by an enormous booming crash of thunder, triggering the birds to take flight from the safety of the trees.

Everyone was in disbelief at my mother's passing. Herbert wailed like the actor he was, but I had to stay strong for my little brothers John and Alfie. I held back my tears and hugged the boys during the funeral whilst the rain pelted down on the Chapel roof and battered onto the windows. Thankfully, the storm was short lived, and we could hear the thunder moving quickly off into the distance.

It had been decided by Herbert's mother, Mrs Flitch, that to save calling the minister out twice and by so doing, cutting costs, the baby would be baptised at the same time as the funeral.

When Mam was pregnant, we talked about the baby and both of us hoped that it would be a girl. If it was, then her name would be Claudette after the film star. We liked fancy names, and both thought that the name Claudette sounded beautiful, very French and sophisticated.

Mrs Flitch had other ideas and the baby was named Olive. Now you know why I was so furious — my mother's last wish was to call her baby, my sister, Claudette but Herbert's mother had decided that this was too fancy a name, which would lead to the child thinking she was better than she was. I thought this was utter rubbish, but not much heed was given to anything I thought in my family, where it seemed that Herbert's mother now made all the decisions.

The service was brief, just a hymn and a prayer. To me it did not matter. Nothing mattered. My mother, Louisa, had died at only thirty-three years of age and she should not have.

Following the two short services of a funeral and a baptism, we emerged from the chapel into early autumn sunshine. The country air smelt of earth and leaves, fresh and clean following the storm.

It was only then that I noticed the unusual sight of a car parked on the village green. There were only two car owners in Little Laxlet in 1931 and they were Dr Blackwood who needed one for visiting his patients and Sir Simeon Styles who was a Justice of the Peace. The baker called once a week in his van but apart from the occasional car passing through and the twice weekly bus, we didn't see many vehicles.

The car on the green was shiny and maroon in colour (I later discovered that it was a Ford Model A) and it belonged to my Aunt Vera and her husband Angus. Vera and Mam had had a falling out about seven years earlier, about the time when Herbert married into the family, so I hadn't seen them since. They said that they had seen the death notice in the Gazette, so she and Angus had come to pay their respects.

Vera, who was tall and striking, looked elegant in her black costume, matching hat with a tiny net veil and fox fur. She wore gloves and I noticed that the handbag she carried looked expensive. Angus wore a dark double-breasted suit and a trilby hat, which made them look the prosperous couple that they were and I felt very much the poor relation, which I was.

I was only eight years old when I last saw them, but Vera hugged me as if it was yesterday. She smelt of perfume, which I later discovered was Arpege by Jeanne Lanvin, which was lovely.

I was small for my age and in mid-hug I realised that the head of the fox was level with my face which I found somewhat disconcerting, as I was eyeball to eyeball with a fox and looking into his glass eyes. We had two things in common, the fox and I, he was as dead as I felt inside, and we shared the same hair colour.

Vera and Angus lived in the iron and steel town of Ransington, about twenty miles from our village. I introduced them to John and Alfie but I had to go back to our cottage as Alfie had wet his pants and the baby needed her bottle.

Before my mother had died, she used to have a job as a cleaner at the 'Shoulder of Mutton' pub in Little

Laxlet. She said it was to put food on the table and shoes on our feet.

Herbert was a work-shy drunkard, so Jim, the landlord had paid Mam's wages directly to her. Herbert did work from time to time as a farm labourer, but it was spasmodic, as were his wages. Luckily Louisa had taken out a penny life insurance policy which covered the cost of the funeral, enabling a proper grave with a headstone in a proper cemetery.

Following the internment there would be food in a private room at the 'Shoulder of Mutton,' courtesy of Jim who had always had a soft spot for my mother.

He would say to her quite regularly, "Louisa will you marry me?"

But she wouldn't, perhaps she thought, he did not mean it.

I used to wish and wish that she had married Jim and I would say to her, "Mam, I think Jim is sweet on you."

She would laugh and reply, "I know he is, but I don't fancy him like that."

I wasn't sure what she meant at the time.

I could never understand what she saw in Herbert Flitch, but she said, "He makes me laugh, he likes to dance and when he plays his fiddle at the pub it makes for a happy party atmosphere."

Too much party if you ask me.

She was three months pregnant with John when they married. Herbert must have swept her off her feet with his fiddle playing and flattery!

After the funeral, I looked after the boys back at the cottage. I kept the fire going and fed the baby her bottle. Mrs Flitch came back at about five o'clock with Vera and Angus.

She said to me, "Take the boys to play on Cuthbert's field."

I just knew that she wanted to talk to Vera and Angus about something that she did not want me to hear. My instincts were absolutely accurate!

Vera and Angus had been married for about ten years and they were childless.

In the privacy of Groat cottage they discussed with Mrs Flitch the possibility of adopting baby Olive. Mrs Flitch thought this to be an excellent idea as it would mean one less mouth to feed and less work for her. She insisted that she needed to ask her Herby, as she called him.

So she left Vera and Angus with the baby and went to look for Herbert in the pub. She returned within ten minutes to say that they could adopt the baby but they needed to leave straight away. Vera suggested that perhaps I, John and Alfie might want to say goodbye, but this was discounted by Mrs Flitch because she said, that she thought it might be too upsetting.

By the time I returned home with the boys, which was about an hour later, all had been agreed and baby

Olive had gone in the maroon Ford Model A with Vera and Angus to their home in Ransington.

I could not believe it and my anger spilled over. I told Mrs Flitch that I thought she was a horrible old witch and that her precious son was a drunken layabout who had married my mother because she was pretty, hard-working and had a bit of cash put by. I knew this to be true, but I also realised that I was being cheeky and provocative.

Her face went puce as her whole countenance flared with temper. She then slapped me hard across my face causing me to fall back, hitting my head on the wall. My face was smarting and as I regained my balance, I saw her reaching for the poker to hit me. I was too quick for her and I darted into the kitchen as the poker hit the wall with a loud crash. It took out a lump of plaster before falling onto the sofa smearing soot all over Mam's lovely cushions. Mrs Flitch might have bad knees and legs, but her arms had the strength of ten men that day.

My heart was pounding as I ran upstairs whilst she was screaming and shouting obscenities after me.

"Betty Dawson, you're a useless, ungrateful wretch and certainly not wanted in this house!" My mother had called me Bettina and I hated being called Betty. She then yelled up the stairs, "Tomorrow I'll find out about putting you in the workhouse because that's where you belong. You are an orphan Betty Dawson, an orphan,

15

and I hope you know what that means, scrubbing floors is all you're fit for!"

I shut myself in my bedroom, away from her rage. Pushing my chest of drawers against the back of the door, my face was throbbing and I could feel a bump on the back of my head and then I cried. But not for long as I realised that to escape would be my only salvation.

CHAPTER TWO

The Telephone Box

"Cooee! Cooee!" It was Hilda, our lovely next-door neighbour, who must have heard the commotion when Mrs Flitch and I were screaming and shouting at each other and as the poker slammed against the party wall.

Hilda and her husband Burt had lived next door to us for all my life and they were kind, good people. Burt had returned from the Great War badly injured and blind. Hilda had told me that the gas the enemy used had damaged Burt's lungs. They had no children of their own, but seemed to enjoy spending time with my brothers and me.

Our cottage was tiny, and I could hear the conversation between Hilda and Mrs Flitch through the gaps in the floorboards of my bedroom.

"Oh Hilda," Mrs Flitch said, "I'm that stressed pet, what with the funeral and Vera taking the baby, thank goodness you've come round. Can you keep the boys for a bit? Just to give me a break. Bettina has got a right mood on her and she is no help at all."

"What do you mean, taken the baby?" Hilda asked in a shocked tone.

"Oh, she's just gone with them for a little holiday. They could see the strain I'm under," lied Mrs Flitch.

Hilda then said, "John and Alfie can stay the night with us if that would help."

Mrs Flitch replied, "That would be just grand Hilda, very helpful I'm sure. I can feel one of my heads coming on, even as we speak, and it's no wonder, I've been on my feet all day and you know how much I suffer with my legs."

Hilda took the boys back to her cottage and five minutes later Mrs Flitch walked briskly along to the 'Shoulder of Mutton'.

Good, I thought, this gives me time to plan. Whilst thinking about what I could do and where I could go my thoughts began to drift back to how things used to be before Herbert Flitch entered our lives.

It used to be just Mam and I living in our lovely little cottage which Jim, the landlord of the pub owned and she rented from him. It was only a two up-two down, with a small back yard, but it was home and we were happy. When the electricity board connected power to the village Jim had it installed in the cottage for us. The big pole was just outside and on quiet nights the wires would make a humming sound which reassured me that even though we were country folk we had moved with the times.

Little Laxlet was as pretty a place as anyone could wish to live in, being a small village, not much more than a hamlet with stone houses of various architectural designs surrounding the village green. Most of the houses had front gardens with stone walls, on which all manner of plants and ferns randomly took root making the walls their home. The gardens themselves were an abundant mix of flowers and vegetables, a style of gardening which I understood to be 'cottage gardening'. The village green was our playground and the huge beech tree in one corner was perfect for climbing, hiding and listening to the conversations of those waiting at the bus stop.

I used to think that it would be a luxury to have running water, but instead there was a white enamel pail with a lid, which we filled with clean water from an outside tap adjacent to the pub. Often Jim carried the water for us, when it was just the two of us.

The toilet, if you can call it that, was an outside earth closet or privy. To get to it you left the front door of the cottage, went along the path then down a passage; at the end of the passage were four doors, behind each was a privy — one for each cottage.

My mother regularly put cold ashes from the fire into the privy to keep the smell down and she whitewashed the walls every spring. For light, we had a candle and there were newspaper squares hanging on a nail. At night we did not use the outside privy as there was a chamber pot beneath each bed. I always thought that my chamber pot was quite beautiful with a green frog sitting on a lily pad inside it.

The kitchen midden was also down the outside passage and it gave off a terrible stench, especially when the weather was hot. There were plenty of spiders and it wasn't unusual to see a rat scuttling about and digging in the rotting rubbish. It was always a good day when the midden men came to empty the midden and the privies. An arduous task for them but executed with, what I considered to be, great fortitude.

Best of all, I loved it when my mother told me about my dad Alfred Dawson, who was the most handsome man she had ever seen in the whole world. He had gorgeous big, brown eyes with thick, dark lashes and hair, almost, but not quite ginger, more rusty brown, with a deep wave, which used to annoy him, but she loved it.

They had met at the village Harvest Supper in the autumn of 1915 and quickly fell in love. They were both seventeen years old at the time and Alfred knew that he would be joining up as a soldier the following February when he would be eighteen years old. He would probably be posted to France or Belgium like his two older brothers, to fight for his country in 'Kitchener's Army'.

On Alfred's birthday, February 14th 1916, he and Louisa were married in Burside parish church. She wore an ankle length dress made from white brocade with three quarter sleeves and a wide, white satin sash. Her dress had a trim of handmade lace around the neck and cuffs. Louisa's wedding shoes were white kid with a narrow strap and a pearl button; her stockings were silk with dots as it was such a special occasion. The wedding veil was exquisite, made from handmade Irish lace and had been worn by Letticia Ann, mother of the bride, on her wedding day, so the veil became the 'something borrowed'.

The 'something blue' was a garter which Vera gave to Louisa on the day. Vera and Agatha (Alfred's younger sister) were bridesmaids and they were both wearing similar dresses in a pale blue stripe with matching hats.

The bridal bouquet was a large bunch of snowdrops which young Agatha had picked on that cold, frosty, wedding day morning. Alfred looked very smart in his army uniform and he wore a small bunch of snowdrops in his buttonhole.

Following the service, the wedding party went to Mr Sempra's Studio for the photographs to be taken. A small wedding reception for the guests was held at the Dawson's farm in Little Laxlet. The food was plentiful and of good quality but there was no music or alcohol as Mr and Mrs Dawson were chapel folk.

Louisa and Alfred spent one night together as husband and wife beneath the thatch of the attic bedroom in the farmhouse. Their brief honeymoon lacked luxury, but they experienced a desire and passion which surprised and delighted them both. The touch of each other's nakedness brought them joy, her flesh against his, their breath and bodies as one, making love and reaching heights of pleasure which amazed and

21

brought ecstasy to them both. Unsurprisingly, Mam would often become quite tearful at the memory of that day and night.

The following day Alfred took 'The King's Shilling' and left for a short period of training before being shipped to France. Although he felt sad at leaving his lovely Louisa, he felt happy in the knowledge that, should he be killed, she would receive a war pension.

Nine months later I was born, but my dad did not see me until he was demobbed in 1918 and I was two years old. Whilst he was away fighting in the war Louisa had settled in Little Laxlet and took the tenancy on Groat Cottage. She had a good friend in Agatha and the Dawson's were kind people, although Mrs Dawson became very depressed when Alfred's two older brothers Joseph and James were both killed in action at the Battle of Passchendaele.

Of course, Louisa was thrilled when Alfred came home even though he was very thin and suffering from foot rot and shell shock. He had night terrors and she would have to try to calm him which was deeply upsetting for them both. His health seemed to improve, even working back on his family farm for a while, but then he caught Spanish Flu after they went with Agatha to the fair at Burside and although everything was tried, to save him, he died five months after coming home.

I cannot remember my dad except that I have seen a photograph of him and Louisa on their wedding day and I will always have her memories.

No more dreaming about the past; as time was of the essence and I knew what I needed to do. Hidden under a loose floorboard in my bedroom I had some money. Keeping it for a rainy day had been Mam's idea; hiding it had been mine. If I ever helped her with the cleaning at the pub, which I did more and more when she was pregnant with the boys and the new baby, then Jim would give me pocket money, which I mostly saved.

I lifted the floorboard and removed some of the money. I then went downstairs to hunt in the sideboard drawer where I knew Mam had kept a book which had important addresses in it.

Fearful that Mrs Flitch might return at any moment I was all fingers and thumbs and found nothing. My palms were sweating and the drawer, aptly named 'the miscellaneous drawer' was just a jumble of all sorts of stuff tangled together. After what seemed an eternity, I found what I was looking for, which was an address book, and tore out the page I needed.

It was very dark outside, except for the pub which was fully lit with sounds of a party in full swing. There were no streetlights in Little Laxlet which worked in my favour as I did not wish to be seen.

As I walked towards the beech tree on the village green and the new concrete telephone box with its red window frames, it seemed like a beacon of hope and a feeling of strength surged within me. Never having used a telephone before I felt slightly anxious, but I had been told that the operators were really helpful, which gave me confidence.

Once inside the box, the instructions on the well-lit notice board above the telephone read, 'Pick up the receiver then dial 0 to speak to an operator' and that was what I did.

A voice said, "Operator speaking, how may I help you?"

I explained that I needed to speak to my Auntie Vera, but I didn't have her telephone number and that I had not used a telephone before.

The operator sounded kind and said, "If you have her address then please give it to me and I will try to find her number for you."

I told her it was Mr and Mrs Angus Mcleod, Iona House, Park Crescent, Ransington.

I waited.

"The number you require is 89606," the operator said, "but it is out of this area so I will have to connect you. Please put three pennies in the slot. If someone answers press button A. If no one answers, then press button B and your money will drop into the metal cup. You may need to put more money in if you hear a pip, pip sound. I'm putting you through now."

There was a ringing tone and a man's voice said, "89606 Angus Mcleod speaking."

I'd already put my pennies into the slot so I now pressed button A. I then babbled on about what had happened with Mrs Flitch and how scared I was.

I then said, "I'm sorry Uncle Angus but I forgot to say that it's me Bettina."

Angus said, "I'll go and fetch your Auntie Vera."

This seemed to take ages and the telephone started pip pipping, so I put three more pennies in the slot.

Vera sounded het up and frazzled when she came to the telephone, but she listened to me and I could tell she was interested and that she couldn't believe that Mrs Flitch had behaved so badly. I found it very reassuring to be talking to her.

I asked how baby Olive was and Vera replied that the baby was very unsettled and crying more than she thought a baby should be crying. I suggested that it had been a very unusual day for them both and perhaps that could be the explanation. I hoped that this would make her feel better.

I then asked, "Have you winded the baby after her feed? If she has wind she will cry."

Vera answered, "I don't know anything about winding, but she has been sick."

I went on to explain how to wind a baby and that it needed to be done halfway through a feed and at the end of the feed.

There was a pause.

Vera then said, "Would you like to come and stay with us for a while?"

I did not hesitate. "Yes please," I said, "but how will I get to your house?"

Vera replied, "Uncle Angus will collect you at nine a.m. tomorrow morning and don't worry about Mrs Flitch, Angus will deal with her."

I put the receiver back on its cradle and pressed button B and a penny dropped into the little container. With my money safe in my pocket I skipped back to the cottage and crept upstairs. Herbert and his mother were still at the pub and John and Alfie were with Hilda next door so I could get on with what I had to do.

I packed some clothes into a bag, along with the rest of my money from under the floorboards. I found my mother's special box which contained important things and I took out my birth certificate just in case I needed it. Then I saw the wedding photograph wrapped lovingly in tissue paper along with my dad's war medal and I wanted them to keep forever. I thought to myself that these things should rightfully be mine and Louisa and Alfred would want me to have them so, after carefully replacing the box, I packed the wedding photograph and the medal in my bag with my money.

My face felt tender and sore from where Mrs Flitch had hit me and there was a bump on the back of my head. I was still fearful for my safety, which was why I pushed the chest of drawers back behind my closed bedroom door. I didn't undress, I kept the light on, and lay on my bed knowing that I would not sleep but I had a crossword book which would help to pass the time until morning.

CHAPTER THREE

Iona House

Not so violent now, the Flitch was snoring loudly in her alcove bed as I prepared to leave Groat Cottage the following morning.

It appeared that Herbert, as usual, had had 'one over the eight' and he'd only made it as far as the sofa last night where he now lay, sprawled out on his back, mouth open with soot from the cushion smeared all over his face.

Once again, I couldn't help thinking, 'What in the world did my mother ever see in him?'

My birth certificate, Dad's war medal and the wedding photograph were now safely in my bag with some clothes and the money I had saved. As I walked towards the door of the cottage I accidentally on purpose stood on Herbert's top hat and crushed it, the resulting sound was immensely satisfying!

I then left.

Outside, the clean country air felt fresh and good on my face. My one and only regret was that I could not take Mam's treadle sewing machine with me. I had glimpsed it on my way out, next to the alcove curtain, with Mrs Flitch's slippers on the treadle and her clothes piled unceremoniously on top.

Uncle Angus met me on the village green at nine a.m. as arranged and I travelled with him in his maroon Ford model A, passing the chapel and the stone houses with their pretty cottage gardens and out of Little Laxlet, towards the bustling iron and steel town of Ransington.

The car interior smelt of leather and I felt safe sitting next to Angus, so I decided to relax and enjoy the journey. The fields and hedgerows slipped by. We passed the army camp and then the landscape became more urban with rows of shops, big churches and the town hall. I reflected that in less than twenty-four hours I had used a telephone and was now being driven in a car, both for the very first time.

Breath-taking was my emotion when I first glimpsed Iona House as it was such an imposing Victorian building with castellations, gargoyles and a tower. The house, surrounded by gardens with rolling lawns and impeccable flower beds, overlooked a park with shrubs and trees offering the property privacy from the road. It was hard for me to believe that I would know anyone who lived in such a house, let alone be related to them.

As we alighted from the car, the luscious perfume from the red climbing rose surrounding the door assailed my senses for a moment, but this was immediately outweighed by the piercing sound of a baby crying loudly, Angus and I rushed straight into the house.

Vera was pacing up and down the hall with baby Olive in her arms. We did not say a word, she just handed the baby to me and I followed her into the kitchen where there was a lidded jug of cool, boiled water on the table. We poured some of the water into a bottle and Olive drank it down very quickly, confirming that she was both hungry and thirsty.

Vera said, "Mrs Flitch instructed me to feed the baby on boiled milk with a teaspoon of sugar added to it."

This obviously hadn't agreed with Olive as she had been vomiting and she would not stop crying. The baby looked exhausted, as did my aunt, and we wondered if Olive might be ill.

Vera said, "There is a new doctor, who has just recently opened a practice not far from here. I think he has a surgery and no appointment is needed. Do you think we should take her around there?"

I replied, "I don't think she is ill, but it would be prudent to have her checked over by a doctor."

My knowledge of bottle feeding was very scanty as we had all been breast fed and Mam had even managed to breast feed baby Olive for two weeks before she died.

The new doctor was Dr Moshe Salmanowicz. We walked to his surgery, which was in the front room of his house, pushing the baby in her magnificent, brand new, shiny black Silver Cross pram.

Dr Salmanowicz had a charming manner and he took us straight into his consulting room. He was dressed in plus-fours with argyle patterned socks and a matching tie. In the cuffs of his cream shirt I noticed that he wore gold cufflinks. His handlebar moustache had waxed ends which fascinated me but the thing I noticed most was that he had kind, twinkly eyes.

Vera explained our circumstances to him and how she had come to have a baby and a teenage girl in her care. I was then introduced to him and calmly but sincerely, he offered me his condolences for my mother.

Olive was then gently lifted out of her pram by Dr Salmanowicz and placed on his medical couch. All the time during the examination, he sang, what sounded like a lullaby, in his native tongue which Olive seemed to enjoy as she focused her gaze on his face and she did not cry at all. I wondered if his moustache held as much a fascination for her as it did for me.

With loud exuberance for such a quiet man, which took Vera and I by surprise he pronounced, "Olive requires Dr Lieburg's formula. She is hungry but otherwise perfectly well."

"Dr Lieburg's formula," Vera repeated. I knew that she was thinking, 'Sounds foreign to me,' but she did not say a word.

"Yes," said Dr Salmanowicz. "It can be bought from my pharmacy, which is in what would otherwise be my kitchen."

The pharmacy cum kitchen was immaculate with the various jars and bottles all arranged on open shelves in an orderly fashion. Near the sink was an area where the doctor mixed his own medicaments such as salves, unctions, tonics and other medicines.

Vera purchased the formula from Dr Salmanowicz who then escorted us to the front door. He said to bring baby Olive back should there be any further problems and that he always had a good stock of Dr Lieburg's formula. We thanked him, he gave a small bow and we said goodbye.

His accent fascinated me as, coming from a small village, I had not met anyone from abroad before. As we walked home Vera explained that he was from Poland and that he had come to live in England for his own safety and that he was a refugee. She then went to explain to me what being a refugee meant and she told me that Ransington now had a small but growing Polish community.

The baby enjoyed her first bottle of Dr Lieburg's formula, so much so, that I do believe she smiled afterwards, but it could have been wind. However, she must have felt full and contented because she fell asleep soon after she had finished her bottle.

Whilst Olive slept, Vera and I had a good chat over a cuppa. She wanted to hear every detail about the incident with Mrs Flitch. When I told her what had happened, she was visibly shocked, and said that it was an appalling way for a grown woman to behave.

I think Vera tried then to lighten the mood saying, "I wonder if they've woken up yet or if they even realise that you've gone?"

She thought it was very funny when I told her that I'd crushed Herbert's top hat; accidentally of course! We both had a fit of the giggles and I was pleased to see her smile.

Iona House was just as interesting inside as it was out and as Vera showed me around there were so many rooms that I quickly lost count. There was a room which had doors opening onto the back garden and another with doors leading into a conservatory, full of huge plants; a kitchen, a scullery and a hall big enough to hold a dance in. Off the hall was a cloakroom with a flush toilet and another toilet next to the coal house, which was accessed from the garden.

Upstairs, there were seven bedrooms and three bathrooms. One bathroom even had a hooded bath with holes in the hood from which water could spray. In each bathroom, there was a hand basin as there was in each bedroom and next to each bathroom, there was a flush toilet made from beautiful patterned ceramic with a mahogany seat.

The thought of having a bath in a proper bathroom with hot and cold running water had me thinking that it must be like a little piece of heaven.

I said, "I love your house Auntie Vera. But how on earth do you manage to keep it looking so lovely. It's huge, there must be such a lot of work?"

She replied, "Mrs Handyside comes in to do cleaning twice a week and Mrs Scribbins comes in to do the washing on a Monday. I also quite enjoy a bit of housework and I love to cook."

My jaw dropped at the thought of having someone come in to help with the cleaning and the washing.

In every room there was an electric bell which relayed to the kitchen where the bell box on the wall showed the room of origin. A servant would then have gone to that room to see what was required. Vera and Angus did not have servants, but my imagination was now working overtime and I just knew that in my next fantasy there would be bells and servants pandering to my every whim.

"Would you like to see your room?" Vera asked. "It overlooks the front garden and Angus and I want you to know that our home is your home for as long as you need it to be."

"That is very kind of you and Uncle Angus," I said.

But I felt that she held something back. So, I decided to ask her straight out.

"Auntie Vera can I ask you something?" I said. "Why did you and Mam fall out? You used to be so close when I was little. It seemed such a shame."

We sat on my new bed with its pink sateen eiderdown and she told me.

"It was all because of Herbert Flitch. When Louisa and Herbert met, she seemed to be enthralled by him and his flattering ways. She brought him here to this house so we could meet him. They came by themselves on the train and when I asked where you were, she told me that, Hilda, her next-door neighbour was looking after you for the day.

"Louisa hadn't known Herbert for long, but they looked very much a couple, which made me feel uneasy and I could not quite put my finger on why that was. Needless to say, I took an instant dislike to him, he acted 'the big I am' but I could see that he was an odious worm of a man. However, I did try very hard not to show my feelings.

"When they left, I noticed that a small silver dish, which was always on the hall table, was missing and I immediately knew who had taken it. Angus and I made the decision not to inform the police nor to tell Louisa, but I did write her a letter in which I advised her, as carefully and tactfully as I could, not to rush into marrying Herbert Flitch. I did not think he would make a good honest husband for her or a stepfather for you.

"Louisa could have done so much better for herself; I knew that; but I never heard from her again. My only regret is that I can never have those years back with my sister. it was time lost and I miss her terribly.

"I do, on occasion hear news of Little Laxlet from Sir Simeon Styles who sits on various boards with Angus, so I did know that Louisa had married Herbert and that they had two sons."

We both needed a hug then as we were crying at the sadness of Louisa's death and we both missed her.

CHAPTER FOUR

Catastrophe

Life at Iona House felt good and we were all looking forward to Christmas. Olive was thriving and Vera was a natural mother in every way, she seemed to be content and enjoying motherhood.

I loved my bedroom and considered it to be my special place. I could not help wondering what Mam would have thought if she could see me living in such luxury.

My sixteenth birthday had been in November and Vera had given me some Yardley's lavender toilet water and bath salts. I even had a proper knee hole dressing table with a mirror, which was where I enjoyed sitting to brush my long, brownish — red hair and this was where I kept the wedding photograph propped-up so that I could look at it every day.

The treadle sewing machine was often in my thoughts and how Mrs Flitch now used it as her dumping ground on which she puts all her personal items, when she went to bed in her alcove behind the curtain.

Before Louisa married Herbert Flitch her treadle sewing machine was in daily use. She was very clever, and would make lovely clothes for us both from items of clothing that she had bought at the jumble sale; dresses, blouses and skirts all in the latest fashionable styles. 'Pegs Paper' was a good source for fashion ideas and occasionally we had a Vogue magazine and she could just look at an outfit, then make it. The magazine called it 'Parisian Haute Couture'. I called it 'Clever Louisa'.

One day Mrs Blackwood, the doctor's wife, knocked on the door and asked if we could make her an outfit. She had the pattern. It was for 'beach resort pyjamas', which were considered very smart at the time.

Mrs Blackwood asked Louisa if she would be able to make the outfit for her. This was the beginning of her dressmaking business. Mrs Blackwood was delighted with her beach resort pyjamas, telling us that she and her husband would be going to Le Touquet in France for a holiday and that the outfit would be perfect.

Word spread about Louisa's skill and the treadle sewing machine was soon working overtime. She was kept busy, but enjoyed being creative and making her clients feel happy. The ladies seemed pleased and Louisa often made the garments extra special with hand embroidered areas on a collar, pocket or cuff. Agatha made beautiful pillow lace and for a special commission they would work together, creating outfits so lovely, often a wedding dress, that the recipient would be near to tears with emotion, as also would be the mother of the bride.

I loved helping whenever I could, the three of us working together, cutting out, pinning, tacking and finishing. The favourite part for us was when the ladies looked happy and pleased with their outfits. Often mam would have some left-over fabric which her clients said she could keep. This would be made up into a frock or a blouse for herself, for me or for Agatha.

It was all going so well until Herbert entered our lives. He did not make a big show of objecting to the dressmaking business, he was more subtle than that. Herbert was adept at creating negativity, especially when he thought that my mother should be making his tea or listening to how he had idled away his day.

Our cottage was small, and Herbert Flitch did not like to see fabric and patterns on the table which meant that we had to be clearing it away all the time. The ladies who used to call for Louisa's dressmaking gradually stopped coming — they obviously felt uncomfortable in such an atmosphere. In a nutshell, his disparaging behaviour spelt the end of the dressmaking business.

Louisa's marriage to Herbert was a rushed affair at the registry office with only the two of them present. Witnesses were required, so Herbert just asked two strangers, who happened to be walking past the building, if they would oblige. The first I knew about it was when they came in and announced that they were man and wife. I was very shocked, but she looked happy on the day, so I suppose I had to feel pleased for her. John was born six months after the wedding and Alfie three years later. There were several miscarriages in between.

Once the boys came along, Louisa was kept busy looking after them, so she made out that this was the reason for the dressmaking to stop, rather than hold Herbert to account.

'On the back burner' she called it, in the hope that she could pick it up again when her children were older. Little did she know that that would never happen.

The layettes she made for her babies were gorgeous. Delicate, tiny outfits in soft white fabrics with intricate embroidery. There were flannel nightdresses and tiny hats and even an exquisite white, thread drawn and embroidered christening gown with a lace trim jointly made with Agatha. Mam even knitted little blankets which were beautiful, each with a different animal appliquéd onto it.

Following Louisa's marriage to Herbert, Agatha stopped visiting us at Groat Cottage. This was due, not to the fact that she was disabled from her hip problem and had to wear a built up boot, but that Herbert seemed to take twisted pleasure in teasing her unkindly, never missing an opportunity to comment on her limp. He called her Agatha Pigeon and he even told her that she would never have a boyfriend unless it was another pigeon, he could be very cruel.

My paternal grandparents, Mr and Mrs Dawson, had given up their farm after my dad, Alfred, had died and they went to live in an old stone house, with the name Providence House, in Little Laxlet with Agatha, where we would often visit them, but it wasn't the same as when she used to come to our cottage when we were all sewing.

The birth of the two boys had been quite straightforward with no complications. As my mother's last pregnancy progressed Mrs Flitch decided that she would move in with us, 'to be around to help' and this she did.

On arrival she announced that she would require a room of her own. This would be difficult in a two up two down cottage, as Louisa and Herbert shared the front bedroom with the boys and I slept in a box back bedroom. The alcove in the living room was designated as Mrs Flitch's space and a curtain was made which pulled across for privacy. As she was supposedly only staying until after the birth, she reluctantly accepted the alcove and then went on to comment that if that was all that was on offer then she supposed it would have to do.

A loud knock on my bedroom door woke me up at about five a.m. that Sunday morning at the end of August 1931.

"Get dressed quickly Betty (I hated being called Betty) and run along and wake Mrs Barnett. It looks like it's Louisa's time. Now hurry yourself up!" shouted Mrs Flitch.

Mrs Barnett was the local woman who delivered babies. She was not a doctor or a midwife, not even a nurse, but she had delivered most of the babies in Little Laxlet and did not cost as much as the doctor. Mrs Barnett looked after Louisa well and at eleven ten a.m. my sister was born weighing 7lb 1oz. The baby was beautiful, and she fed straight away. Mam and I were both pleased to have a girl after two boys.

When the baby was three days old Louisa started to say that her left leg felt hot and tingling and she could not feel her left foot. The leg looked pale and swollen and I wanted Dr Blackwood to be called to check her over and look at the swollen leg.

Mrs Flitch said, "No Betty, Louisa is just tired and needs a poultice and more rest."

As the days went on Mam's leg became more painful and Mrs Flitch kept insisting that more bandaging and rest were all that was needed. My mother had what was known as White Leg.

Two weeks after the baby was born, Herbert was up early which was most unusual. I was making the porridge on the range trivet for everyone and Mrs Flitch was sitting with her feet up, reading the paper.

"Where are you off to son?" she asked him.

"Oh, just out, there might be a job going. Dickie Pearson knows about it so I'm going to see him."

I thought, 'Job my eye, he'll be going to ask Dickie Pearson to put a bet on for him in town. If there is a job it'll be something dodgy.'

"Is Mam awake?" I asked him, thinking that she might be ready for a cuppa.

"No, she's asleep still," said Herbert, as he went out of the door.

The baby, who was upstairs, then started to cry and she did not stop. I was dishing out the breakfast for everyone so Mrs Flitch, grumbling, heaved herself out of her chair and went upstairs to investigate.

Two weeks following the birth of a healthy baby girl my mother had died of a pulmonary embolism which is a blood clot. It had been in her leg and travelled to her heart causing her death. Had Herbert even taken the time to notice that his wife was dead and not sleeping? That I doubted very much.

Mrs Flitch had, what I considered, a very abrupt and uncaring manner as she came downstairs and broke the news, shouting, "Your mam is dead! Look after the boys whilst I go and find my Herby."

Dr Blackwood was called to the cottage where he confirmed my mother's death. Mrs Barnett was then sent for to lay her out. I think, at that point, I just closed down emotionally, until after the funeral.

However, the new baby needed care and the boys were quite demanding, so I was kept busy, which was probably a good thing. Herbert and his mother focused on cashing in the insurance policy. Life is full of 'if only's' but if only I'd insisted on calling the doctor when my mother was alive then things might have been different. In that house at that time no one had any interest in me or anything I might have to say. In other words, I felt as though I had no voice.

My thoughts now returned to the treadle sewing machine and how much I would love to have it at Iona House. Olive was now almost four months old and I kept thinking of all the pretty dresses I could make for her.

Today, Vera and Angus are having an important meeting with their solicitor regarding adopting Olive; a private adoption I was told, was quite a straightforward procedure in 1931, requiring only the consent of the parent or guardian, then the necessary papers go to the Court where the adoption is confirmed and legalised.

When they returned from seeing their solicitor Vera seemed worried.

She said, "Oh Bettina, the solicitor says it looks quite a straightforward adoption and it should all be through by the end of January next year, but he does not know Herbert Flitch and his mother. Do you think they will put a spanner in the works?"

I tried to reassure her, but deep down, I could not help feeling the same.

CHAPTER FIVE

Sophie to the Rescue

It was one week before Christmas. I was helping Vera make the Christmas puddings and we felt happy and relaxed even though she said that all the preparations were late this year. We dropped silver three penny bits into the pudding mixture and everyone, including Mrs Scribbins and Mrs Handyside, made a wish whilst giving it a good stir. Once the puddings were steaming on the stove, we sat at the table in the warm, happy kitchen with a cup of tea and a mince pie. Olive gurgled in her pram; it was such a lovely afternoon.

"Ho! Ho! Ho!" shouted a voice through the back door. When we looked it was Angus with a huge Christmas tree.

"You must have smelt the mince pies Angus. What a magnificent tree, perfect for the hall. Come on in out of the cold," Vera said as she poured him a cup of tea and put a mince pie on his plate.

When Angus entered the kitchen, he went straight to the pram and picked Olive up. He chatted to her and she cooed back — happiness was palpable that afternoon.

The telephone rang in the hall and I answered it.

"89606 Bettina speaking," I said in my best telephone voice.

I was becoming quite confident with the telephone now and enjoyed the responsibility of answering it. Beside the phone was a notepad and pen which I would use to write down a message for Angus or Vera if they were unavailable to take the call.

The voice on the telephone sounded upset; it was Hilda.

"Bettina pet," Hilda said, 'I'm sorry to bother you but it's John and Alfie. My Burt has taken really poorly, and I can't have them here with me any more." Hilda then went on to explain that they had been staying with her since the funeral and now that her husband was so poorly, she could not manage to look after him and the boys.

The pips pipped and we were cut off.

I returned to the kitchen and told Vera and Angus, who were both as shocked and surprised as I was that John and Alfie had been staying with Hilda and Burt for so long.

"Why that must be more than three months," Vera said, "Where are Herbert and Mrs Flitch? Surely they should be looking after them."

Angus said, "Well there's nothing else for it, I'll just have to go to Little Laxlet and try to find out what's going on. Whilst I'm there I will remind Herbert about signing the adoption papers for Olive. He seems to be dragging his feet."

'Good luck with that,' I thought.

The sky was clear, and it was very frosty when Angus left for the village the following morning.

I could see that Vera was anxious about the icy roads as she hugged him and said, "Please take care."

As the maroon Ford Model A, drove away from Iona House and turned into the road we waved, both hoping he would be safe. It was such a cold and wintry morning, that we could see our breath — so we quickly returned indoors.

On arrival at Little Laxlet Angus went straight to Groat Cottage and he knocked on the door, in what he hoped was a firm but not unfriendly manner.

Mrs Flitch greeted Angus on the doorstep with a hostile, "What do you want?"

Angus then explained the reason for his visit and her response was, "None of your business, nothing to do with you."

It was freezing standing on the doorstep but not as icy as her welcome. The door was then shut in his face.

At the next-door cottage Hilda was more welcoming, and Angus was offered a cup of tea. Burt now had a bed in the living room beside the window and Angus could see that the man was very ill.

"Do you know where John and Alfie are?" Angus asked.

"I'm not sure where they are," Hilda replied. "I took them back home last night and I haven't seen them since."

Angus thanked Hilda for the tea and said that he hoped her husband would feel better soon. This was a faint hope as the gas damage from the war to Burt's lungs was causing great difficulty with his breathing.

Perhaps Jim, at 'The Shoulder of Mutton' might be able to throw some light onto the whereabouts of the two boys. However, Angus did not have a good feeling about the whole situation; two very young children missing on an extremely cold December day.

Jim welcomed Angus although they did not know each other well, having only met once before at Louisa's funeral. Jim knew that the boys had been living with Hilda and he also knew that Burt now had a bed downstairs because he had brought the bed down with his friend Harry. It was now after midday and the bar was open, Angus half expected to see Herbert Flitch propping it up, but he wasn't there.

Jim told Angus that Herbert did not frequent the 'Shoulder of Mutton' much these days and had heard that he now drank at 'The Fox and Hounds' in Great Laxlet, which was the next village. He did not like to mention that Herbert was now courting the barmaid from that hostelry.

Louisa's insurance had paid out more than expected so Herbert was now flush with cash, but no doubt it would soon drain away.

Jim then went along to Groat Cottage and he knocked at Mrs Flitch's door.

He was told by her, "No I do not know where the boys are."

From her attitude and the aggressive look on her face Jim gathered that she did not know where they were, nor did she care.

Harry, Jim's friend, was happy to look after the pub whilst Angus and Jim searched the outbuildings and yards. After an hour of searching they were joined by several other men, Harry had told every man who went into the pub that the boys were missing and all of them wanted to help. Some men had brought dogs trained to the gun, who also sometimes searched for missing walkers out on the fell.

Hilda could see the search party gathering near the pub and she offered a jumper, which belonged to John, to give a scent for the dogs. The search party spread out, going through all the farm buildings, fields, barns and hedgerows, even going along the riverbank and looking into the swirling, swollen, torrid river. The whole village of Little Laxlet was searched but the boys were not to be found.

More people now joined the search party and it was decided to spread the search further afield. On the edge of the next village, Great Laxlet, there was an old disused army depot which had been used for storage of armaments during the Great War. The building, now overgrown with ivy and nettles, was dilapidated, vandalised and considered unsafe.

As the search party approached this building the dogs became excited, barking as a signal to enter the old depot. It was mid-afternoon and beginning to get dark when a red spaniel named Sophie found the boys. She bravely went into the building, taking a hazardous route over shards of broken glass, old leaking batteries, barbed wire, sharp nails and other detritus left over from the war. This amazing dog just sat beside the boys and waited for Simon, who was Dr Blackwood's son and her owner. John recognised Sophie and when he spoke to her she immediately moved closer to him and licked his outstretched hand.

The children were numb with cold and they had wrapped some old sacking round their shoulders to keep warm. Alfie was almost unconscious, and John was ashen, his lips were blue, and he was crying.

John said, through chattering teeth, "Dad is in The Fox and Hounds, he bought us pop and crisps and he told us to sit on a bench in the pub garden till he came back for us." He added, "It became too cold to wait on the bench, so we decided to walk back home. We got lost and Alfie wanted Mam. We were very cold, so we came in here. We thought we'd have a little rest then try again to go home. But Alfie fell asleep."

John was extremely upset, and he was crying loudly now and saying that he was sorry, but he could not have left Alfie on his own. The child was very frightened and worried that he would be in trouble.

Angus thanked the search party and the dogs, especially Sophie and Simon. Then he and Jim picked the boys up and carried them back to the 'Shoulder of Mutton'. Jim's living quarters, upstairs in the pub, had a cosy fire in the grate and the boys soon warmed up. Jim gave them soup and bread whilst Angus went along to tell Hilda that John and Alfie had been found and that they were safe.

Angus then drove his car to 'The Fox and Hounds' pub some three miles away where Herbert was playing his fiddle in the bar, entertaining the other customers who were clapping, singing and generally having a good time. It was now seven p.m. and Angus wondered if Herbert had given any thought to his boys since he had brought them here at lunchtime.

The afternoon had been spent by Herbert and his new girlfriend, Maisie the barmaid, in her attic bedroom upstairs. They had enjoyed such vigorous, voracious sex for over an hour that they fell asleep until it was time for Maisie to open the pub at six thirty p.m.

Angus was not aware of the details of how Herbert had spent his afternoon whilst his boys were freezing and could have died of hypothermia alone in a dangerous, derelict building, which is probably just as well.

The two men met in the bar and Angus suggested to Herbert that they needed to have a private word regarding signing the adoption papers. Herbert brushed him off with the excuse that he was busy, and he did not have the time. He would look at it after Christmas.

Keeping calm at this point was quite difficult for Angus as several other people, including Herbert's new girlfriend, had begun to listen in.

Angus calmly said, "Perhaps such a private conversation as this should be conducted in a less public place."

"No, no, no," Herbert said, "these people are my friends."

"Then," Angus said, "perhaps you would like to tell them where your boys are?"

Herbert's face froze with shock as he had completely forgotten about the boys and immediately realised that he could be arrested for child neglect.

The rest of the conversation regarding John and Alfie and the signing of the adoption papers was conducted in the snug which was much quieter. Under the implied threat of Angus informing the authorities of Herbert's neglect of his children and a possible jail sentence Herbert agreed to sign the papers straight away. Angus had also dropped into the conversation that Sir Simeon Styles the JP was a personal friend.

Angus and Herbert went, by car, to Groat Cottage in Little Laxlet and Herbert went indoors, and brought out the adoption papers to be signed. They then went to the 'Shoulder of Mutton' where Herbert signed the papers and Jim counter-signed as a witness.

Outside again, Angus said, "I will be taking John and Alfie home with me if they want to go."

Herbert's response was, "Okay with me;" nothing more, just "Okay with me".

Herbert then said, "It's freezing out here Angus mate, any chance of a lift back to The Fox and Hounds?"

Angus refrained from punching him, which is what he felt like doing. He just walked away thinking that a three mile walk back to Great Laxlet in the freezing cold would give Herbert Flitch a taste of his own medicine.

The boys agreed that they would like to go and stay with Angus and Vera for Christmas and see Bettina and Olive again, so Jim made them comfortable for the night in one of his letting rooms. John and Alfie soon fell asleep and Angus walked along to the new telephone box by the beech tree on the village green and phoned Vera to give her the news.

She was delighted that the adoption papers were now signed and could now be handed over to their solicitor. At the news of two extra guests for Christmas her response was that it would be wonderful to have the house full of children and that hot water bottles would be put in their beds straight away.

Angus reflected on how lucky he was to have met Vera all those years ago. She had worked in the bank where Angus did business and he always tried to be served by her. After he had met her in the bank a few times he asked her out to go dancing with him and she agreed. They were married within a year, but Vera had to leave her job as a bank teller, because the bank did not employ married women. She had loved her job and although Vera always knew, that as a woman, she would never be promoted to a senior position, she still had enjoyed working as part of a team and serving the public.

As Angus walked back to the pub past the beech tree on the village green, the grass now white with frost, he could not help but think that it had been a very eventful day. He looked up at the night sky which was bright with stars and felt very thankful about the way things had turned out and that the boys were safe. He was also looking forward to sharing a nightcap in the bar with Jim.

CHAPTER 6

Christmas Shopping

It was time for John and Alfie to say goodbye to Little Laxlet for Christmas, so Angus took them to see Hilda and Burt to say 'thank you' for their hospitality. He had also ordered, through Jim, a Christmas hamper, which would be delivered to Hilda and Burt's cottage on Christmas Eve.

In my bedroom at Iona House I counted the money I'd saved, with a view to doing Christmas shopping. There was just enough, but I realised that as soon as it was New Year my main objective would be to find myself a job. I had already mentioned this to Vera who told me that she would talk to Angus and perhaps there might be an opening for me at Landsdown Short where he worked.

I went into town and the big department store glowed with pretty, festive displays of Christmas goods in all shapes and sizes, but to me everything seemed very expensive. The haberdashery and fabric departments were of particular interest and I could not help but think that if only I had a sewing machine and a bit more time, I could easily have made gifts for everyone. Having looked at all the lovely things on sale I decided that the department store was too costly for my budget and so I left.

Wandering further into town, I smelt a delicious aroma, I then came to a corner where a man was selling roasted chestnuts from a metal barrow containing hot coals. One halfpenny bought me a paper bag of delicious roasted chestnuts which I peeled and ate as I started to walk back along the High Street, enjoying window shopping.

The very smell of the chestnuts reminded me of the time when Mam and I had a try at roasting some on a shovel on the open range fire in Groat Cottage. We hadn't realised that the skins needed to be slit before roasting. As the chestnuts became hot, they fired off round the room like bullets which meant that we had to quickly dodge out of the way then hunt for them amongst the furniture. As we peeled and ate them, we laughed, and said that we were lucky not to have been shot. Once Herbert Flitch moved in with us, Christmas was never the same again and there was definitely no more chestnut roasting.

I'd heard from Mrs Handyside that a store called Woolworths was a good place to shop as they offered a huge variety and it was good value for money. I made the decision that this would be the very place to go to if I wanted to buy everyone a gift.

On the wide pavement outside Woolworths there was a row of prams, each containing a baby feeding itself with, what looked like, a bottle of tea. Those too young to hold the bottle themselves had it propped on a cushion and I supposed that if the child was lucky then it would not choke. I counted eight prams in all and not a mother in sight.

I found Woolworths to be a veritable treasure trove with wide aisles and counters packed full of interesting and reasonably priced items.

For John and Alfie, I bought each of them a little tin plate car, one in red and one in green. I bought Olive a pretty woollen bonnet and a little teddy bear; a scarf for Angus and handkerchiefs in a Christmas box for Vera. I lingered over the paper dress patterns but I realised that there was no point in buying one, so I bought a Micky Mouse jigsaw puzzle which I thought might keep the boys busy for a while. I had a quick look at the haberdashery which was equally as good as the department store.

Including some wrapping paper and Christmas cards, my total shopping trip came to three shillings, eleven pence and one halfpenny, which I considered good value for money.

As I began the walk home, I noticed, down a side street, two fisher women selling fish from a cart. The women wore big, colourful cotton bonnets and aprons made from rough cloth and rubber. The fish looked and smelt fresh, so I joined the queue.

A man with a portable barrel organ set up a pitch a few yards from the fish cart. His jaunty manner, bright jacket and bowler hat caught the attention of those of us queuing, as did his monkey.

Before commencing playing he called out to the fisher women, "Morning me bonnie lasses, any requests?"

They ignored him and continued serving their customers.

"Now Mary me darlin, you know how much I'm crazy over ye, this one's just for you."

He started to play 'If You Were the Only Girl in the World'.

"I cannot stand the sight of you Geordie Brown! Go and take your organ round the town hall, play it for t' councillors!" Mary shouted.

"Councillors, skin flints more like, your customers are the salt of the earth and generous with it!" He shouted back, encouraging the monkey to shake the tin. "A special licence would see us married for Christmas me darlin. Just think how nice that would be. You, me and Tinks here."

Tinks, the monkey, was now on Geordie's shoulder, probably frightened by all the shouting.

"Well I've got news for you Geordie, there's no way I'll be living with that bloody monkey of yours so piss off back to Durham and throw yourself in't river," Mary retorted.

"I love it when she gets mad and flushed up, stirs me passion it does," Geordie said to the small crowd which had now gathered.

I bought four fillets of cod dexterously filleted by Mary's companion, whom I understood to be Nancy. As the fish was expertly wrapped in paper she commented, "Don't take a hapeth of notice of those two love birds, we get this all the time."

What a commotion there was when I arrived back at Iona House. Mr Handyside and his son Stan were filling a big tub with soil and putting up the Christmas tree in the hall. There seemed to be an accompaniment of shouting and mess, so I quickly figured out that the best thing for me would be to take my shopping upstairs out of the way. However, I did put the fish on the marble slab in the pantry first.

Vera was upstairs and she seemed very pleased when I told her that I'd bought fish. She told me that the fisher women came to town twice a week on the train from the coast and that the fresh fish was always delicious. She told me that Mary and Geordie always shouted and argued as this worked as a good 'crowd puller' for them.

She said, "Tonight we shall have fish pie for supper, it is one of Angus's favourite meals."

Vera was an excellent cook. We often joked that she could hardly sew a button on, but her cooking skills were fantastic. Louisa had been the stitcher and Vera the cook.

"Do you think the boys will like this room?" Vera asked.

The room was big with twin beds and I assured her that they would love it. We then heard the toot of a car horn and from the landing window we could see Angus, John and Alfie getting out of the car. They had no luggage and the clothes the boys wore looked two sizes too small for them and rather tatty.

By the look on the boys faces I think that they found the big house rather overwhelming. I'd never known them to be so quiet, not ever! Stan and Mr Handyside were still in the hall, the tree was up, and they were tidying away stray pine needles and soil into a dustpan.

Vera was pleased that Angus was safely home, as she had heard on the wireless that cold, icy weather was forecast, and she certainly did not want him driving on frozen country roads.

Angus said, "I really must go into the office today and tie up a few loose ends before the Works close for Christmas."

He had an important job at Landsdown Short, the local iron and steel works. I wasn't exactly sure what it was but I thought it must be important, perhaps he was even a manager. However, I did know that he was an Alderman in the town, which carried a great deal of responsibility.

John and Alfie were silent, even when Stan asked, "Looking forward to Christmas boys? I hope Santa brings you lots of presents."

I said, "I'm sorry, I think the cat got their tongues, they are not usually this quiet."

We all went through into the kitchen where Vera said, "How about sandwiches all round for lunch?"

The boys nodded until I poked them in the back, and they said together, "Yes please."

Mr Handyside and Stan took their sandwiches and mugs of hot strong tea down to the shed where they would be having a discussion regarding the new heating system in the greenhouse.

Mr Handyside looked after the gardens at Iona House, which did not involve much work in December, so he spent most of his time sharpening his tools and planning for the spring and summer. The planning part of his job involved sitting in an old chair in the shed reading the seed catalogues, however Mrs Handyside had already told me how busy her husband would be for the rest of the year.

"You know how it is," she had said, "pushing that heavy mower around and digging the veg. Very hard on the back."

I had replied, "Yes, it is."

Although I had not a clue if it was hard on the back or not as we had only had a little flagged yard at Groat Cottage.

Vera had noticed that all the boys had brought with them were the clothes they were standing up in.

"This afternoon, when Olive has had her bottle, we are all going to walk into town." she said.

John and Alfie looked bewildered, but I guessed that it was to buy them new clothes.

We left the house at about two p.m. and walked purposefully into the town centre. Passing Woolworths, I noticed that there were even more unattended prams containing babies than there had been earlier. We went straight to the department store where no one seemed to object to Olive in her big Silver Cross pram entering the store. Closing time for the store was five thirty p.m., we needed to focus so, without hesitation Vera pressed the button for the lift.

Olive was wheeled in her pram into the lift, which took the lift attendant quite by surprise as he became squashed up against the mahogany panelling.

"Which floor Madam?" he gasped.

"Children's clothing please," Vera instructed, and the now silent attendant pressed the button for the second floor. The boys and I took the stairs and we met Vera and Olive in the Children's department.

Vera sat on a chair with Olive in the pram beside her, whilst the shop assistants brought items of boys clothing for her to see and for my brothers to try for size. Underwear, socks, trousers, jumpers, and a jacket and cap for each. Shirts, pyjamas and dressing gowns, were all for John and Alfie, I quickly lost track of the cost.

We then walked with the pram, negotiating, with help from the staff, the various steps on the way to the Children's Shoe Department. Here John and Alfie had their feet measured and were fitted with shoes. Vera then realised that they did not have slippers, so they each chose a pair in the colour of their choice.

Shopping in style was something I had never experienced in my life and I found this visit to the shops quite extraordinary, almost surreal.

The store manager asked Vera, "Will your purchases be going onto your account Madam?"

"Yes," answered Vera, "And please can it all be delivered by six p.m. this evening?"

"Of course, Madam," he replied.

He did not even ask Vera her name or address so I thought that he must be a friend. Little did I realise at the time the status Vera and Angus had in Ransington, as not only was Angus an Alderman in the town but he was also the Managing Director of Landsdown Short.

Before we left the store, Vera asked me to choose a dress, a cardigan and new shoes for myself. I'd never bought a dress or cardigan before and didn't even know my size. Vera helped me and she suggested that I pop into a changing room to try them on. I was not even sure what a changing room was or where it was but a very nice young lady, not much older than I, was very helpful and she showed me the way.

When I came out of the changing room in my new finery, Vera was sitting on a chair with the big Silver Cross pram beside her and she said, "Oh my word, you look just like Louisa."

She then promptly burst into tears.

Once again, everything was to be put onto the McLeod account and would be delivered to Iona House by six p.m.

We then visited the Baby Department where we chose a gorgeous, pink Viyella dress with smocking for Olive to wear on Christmas Day. It occurred to me that at no time during our shopping trip had Vera even looked at the price of anything and the staff in the store treated her like royalty.

'Could it be,' I asked myself at the time, 'that Angus and Vera are very rich?'

The shopping trip had been the epitome of effortlessness, achieving so much in one afternoon.

Alfie said, "My legs are tired."

Vera scooped him up and sat him in the pram at the handle end for our walk home. Never before had I had such diverse shopping experiences, Woolworths in the morning and the department store in the afternoon, they could not have been more different in terms of personal service.

When we arrived home Vera asked, "Would you and the boys like to decorate the Christmas tree while I make the supper?"

I liked that idea and John and Alfie helped to hang the pretty glass baubles and decorations without breaking anything. No one fell of the stepladder, which was a relief, as John had balanced precariously whilst putting the star on the topmost branch.

Angus arrived home carrying an armful of holly and ivy. He said to the boys, "There's more in the car. Do you want to help me bring it in?"

Both boys seemed keen to help although they were still very quiet.

Later, when we had enjoyed our fish pie supper, I helped Vera to clear away the dishes and Angus disappeared into his study to do The Times crossword. The Times newspaper was delivered daily to Iona House, so he now had two crosswords to do as he had been away collecting John and Alfie the day before.

When Angus was away in Little Laxlet I'd picked up his newspaper from the doormat and had a quick look at the crossword. I did enjoy the challenge of a crossword but that one looked very difficult and I would not have done it anyway; after all it was Angus's paper. So, I smoothed it out and placed it, neatly folded on the desk in his study.

Whilst Vera changed Olive into her night clothes and fed her before bed, I bathed the boys in the big bath which they enjoyed, then washed their hair, which they did not enjoy quite so much. How cute they both looked in their new pyjamas, dressing gowns and slippers. It would have made our mother happy to know that Vera and Angus looked after us so well. I wondered if I would ever be able to repay them for their kindness.

John and Alfie went downstairs to say goodnight to Uncle Angus who was still in his study and then Vera and I tucked them into their cosy beds. The boys were both asleep before I'd even finished telling them their favourite bedtime story and I do not think they even realised that tomorrow would be Christmas Eve.

CHAPTER 7

Christmas Eve 1931

It was a tradition in Ransington for the farmers from outlying areas to bring poultry to the town market to sell on Christmas Eve.

"If we are there very early," Angus said, "we will be certain of bagging a bargain."

He seemed pleased to be having the day doing something which was a total change from the pressures of going into the offices of the iron and steel works.

I wasn't absolutely sure what he meant by 'bagging a bargain' as I knew, because Vera had told me, that he had ordered a goose from Mr Smith who farms out Burside way, not far from Little Laxlet.

Although it was very early and still dark, the market was in full swing when we arrived. The farmers and butchers were all doing a roaring trade. Mr Smith had our goose ready and beautifully packed in a box, along with a large ham. Angus also bought two chickens, one for Mrs Handyside and one for Mrs Scribbins.

A girl's voice said, "Hello stranger."

It was Ada Smith, the farmer's daughter who had been in my class at school. Although we had never been close friends, I always thought she was good fun to be around.

The Smith's stall was very busy, but Ada said, "I'm due a tea break in five minutes, if you're not in a rush it would be great to have a chat."

Angus said that that would be fine, but we would have to leave in about half an hour as Vera might need a hand.

He then went off, whistling, 'Hark the Herald Angels Sing', into the heart of the market where the fruit, nuts and vegetables were. Perhaps he would 'bag a bargain' there.

Holding our mugs of hot tea in our freezing cold hands Ada and I sat together in her dad's van. It was such a cold morning that the heat from the mugs of tea quickly steamed up the windows.

"What's it like living in the town?" Ada asked.

"It's been busy since Mam died," I replied. "The baby, John and Alfie are here now, but the boys will be going back to their dad after Christmas."

Ada said, "I heard about your mother, it's very sad. I'm so sorry." She then went on to say, "My mam was fifty-two when she had me and she is still working on the farm, even now at her age, she seems so old to me. I would much rather have had a young mother and what's more I've decided I won't have any children after I'm twenty-one."

Ada did not seem to be aware that the way the conversation was going was rather insensitive!

To change the subject I asked, "What's going on in Little Laxlet. Any excitement?"

This question was akin to opening the floodgates.

"Have you heard about Herbert Flitch and his goings on?" she asked.

"I'd heard he was courting Maisie at 'The Fox and Hounds', but that's all," I replied.

Ada then became very animated and she hardly drew breath whilst telling me that Maisie's real boyfriend had returned from being away at sea. He was a big, burly sailor with a fearful temper and he had even been in a foreign jail; Shanghai she thought, for fighting and brawling in a bar and a man was killed.

The ship's Captain had to 'spring him' by bribing the jailers with money and rum then, he had to get him back quickly onto the ship more or less as it set sail. Ada thought that the boyfriend was called Fred, but she wasn't absolutely sure about that, but she was sure that he wasn't a man to be crossed.

"Anyway," Ada went on, "He thought he'd surprise Maisie and he even planned to propose to her."

I thought that this story might have a romantic ending, but I was beginning to doubt it!

"He'd bought the ring and everything," Ada said dramatically. "Well, when Fred got to 'The Fox and Hounds' to surprise Maisie, she was in bed and 'at it' with Herbert Flitch."

Ada rolled her eyes expressively! She went on, "Lucky for them the pub wasn't open and the front door was locked. Fred went around the back and the pot man, Sammy, let him in. Maisie had heard voices and she recognised one voice as that of Fred. Fred's footsteps sounded on the stairs.

She frantically said to Herbert, "Get out of here, quick, run for it or he'll kill us both."

Herbert grabbed his clothes and scrambled out of the window, which was three floors up, but luckily for him there was a fire escape and he was down it in a flash, stark naked. More expressive eye rolling.

"Maisie then had to quickly calm herself as she pushed Herbert's boots and her knickers under the bed, before opening the bedroom door to welcome Fred into her outstretched arms and, still warm, bed. His gaze was so fixed on the sight of Maisie's voluminously large breasts with nipples akin to perfect, pink organ stops that his thoughts were of the pleasures to come; so much so he did not even notice the indentation left on the pillow by Herbert Flitch."

"How do you know all this?" I asked.

"Well," said Ada, "Our Molly is walking out with Sammy the pot man and he told her everything. Maisie filled him in with the bedroom details when Fred was on the toilet and she asked Sam to get rid of Herbert's boots. The last Sammy saw of Herbert Flitch was him running across the fields, barefoot and wearing only his long johns."

The thought of such a sight made us giggle.

"Sounds as though Herbert's romance at 'The Fox and Hounds' is over then," I said.

"Oh yes," said Ada, "he's never been seen there since. I reckon he'll be lying low now, at least until Fred goes back to sea."

Angus knocked on the van window and I said goodbye and Merry Christmas to Ada.

The day went by in a flash. The Handyside's called into the kitchen of Iona House for their chicken. Angus offered them a Christmas tot of brandy which Mrs Handyside declined, preferring a cup of tea, but Mr Handyside accepted.

We chatted about Christmas and the weather, then Vera said how excited she was to have children in the house and how much she was looking forward to seeing them open their presents. Her sanguine smile and calm demeanour gave me a feeling of hope that Christmas would be joyful.

Mrs Scribbins called in for her chicken and she said, "I've just come from cleaning at the 'arrison's and they are in a right old pickle. Their water tank 'as burst and the kitchen ceiling is down."

Vera said, "Poor things, how on earth will they manage to cook their Christmas dinner?"

She did not know the Harrisons but from her concerned expression I could see she felt sorry for them.

"Never mind and don't you worry Mrs McLeod," said Mrs Scribbins, "they are well hinsured and I don't mind if I do and a Merry Christmas to you Sir." All in one breath when Angus offered her a brandy.

She then said, "Medicinal, that's right, it'll hease me hartheritis it will. Very kind of you I'm sure. I've just seen the harmy on me way 'ere, I expect they'll be passing the door soon on their way to the park."

Iona House was one of several very large houses which looked onto the park. When the town was built the planners considered that a central park would be of great benefit to the public and they were right, the park was a wonderful open space.

'The lungs of the town' Vera called it. Properties overlooking the park tended to be very grand. It was thought to be one of the best places to live in Ransington — and much sought after.

We heard the band as the army approached and I took John and Alfie into the front garden to watch the parade. However, it was not the military army, as I had expected, but The Salvation Army band. They marched into the park and onto the bandstand, where they prepared for a short concert.

Vera gave us some money and we went into the park to listen to the Christmas carols, the boys put the change into the collection box, and I explained to them that the money was to help the Salvationists provide help for the poor. It was beginning to really feel like Christmas.

When we were back at Iona House, I asked John and Alfie if they were feeling excited about Father

Christmas. They said that they were now, as Auntie Vera had told them that tonight they would be hanging up their stockings and perhaps, if they were very good, in the morning, there would be presents for them.

Later, John and Alfie did hang up their stockings on the big brass rod across the old scullery range before they went to bed. A mince pie and a brandy were left for Father Christmas on the hearth and a carrot for the reindeer.

Angus and Vera looked very contented sitting together in the drawing room, listening to the BBC Symphony Orchestra on the wireless, so I said, "Goodnight."

Angus was doing his Times crossword and Vera was browsing through her Homes and Gardens magazine. It did cross my mind, seeing them sitting together in such a relaxed but almost prim manner that perhaps they had never enjoyed the 'pleasures of the flesh' and that could be the reason why they had never had children. I later discovered this not to be the case; they just did not believe in public displays of affection.

I then went upstairs to my bedroom and wrapped the gifts I had bought in readiness for tomorrow. Once in bed I enjoyed the luxury of reading Vera's latest Vogue magazine. Looking at the fashions, my thoughts turned to Louisa and how much she had enjoyed Vogue. I also allowed my mind to wander back to what Ada had told me about Herbert. If Maisie's boyfriend had killed him, I doubted that anyone would miss him, even for a minute. I knew I certainly would not.

I realised that the boys would be returning to Little Laxlet after Christmas which made me feel very uneasy. The idea of Herbert and his mother looking after them was worrying, but as he was their father, they were his responsibility. He was clueless about parenting and Mrs Flitch did not give a damn. Hilda had told Angus that John had not been back to school since Mam died and although she felt bad about it, she could not leave Burt on his own whilst she walked the two miles there and back.

Our mother had considered education to be very important and as soon as I was old enough, she bought me a bicycle to ride to school, along with the other village children. John had a little bike and he had started to ride with us in the spring of 1931. I left school at age fifteen with the hope of finding a job, but then Mam was pregnant again and so she needed my help. My plan had been to find work as soon as the baby was born, but then she died.

Snuggled under my pink sateen eiderdown, looking at the fashions in Vogue made me think, once again, about the treadle sewing machine in Groat Cottage. Was it still there or perhaps, had Mrs Flitch sold it? Recently I had noticed an advertisement in the Woman and Home magazine, which was also delivered to the house, for a portable, electric sewing machine. This rather took my fancy as I thought it would fit nicely on my knee hole dressing table when I wanted to use it and then it could be stored in its box underneath when I wasn't using it. However, I realised that it was a job that I really needed. This would allow me the ability to earn money and save for a sewing machine of my own.

As I drifted off to sleep, in my imagination, I was making beautiful garments with my new sewing machine.

CHAPTER 8

Christmas Morning 1931

John and Alfie's faces on Christmas morning were a picture of pure surprise and pleasure when they found their stockings full of wonderful surprises. Angus had bought them a train set which was quickly assembled and as we ate breakfast we watched and listened to the sound of the toy trains.

Baby Olive was a very contented baby and she gurgled and laughed at the boys' antics. My gift from Vera and Angus was a small, beautiful gold locket on a chain. Someone, I suspect Vera, had put a picture of Louisa inside it. I knew that this, my first piece of jewellery, would always be precious to me. The house looked wonderful with the impressive Christmas tree, holly and ivy round the picture frames and a fire lit in all the downstairs rooms.

The whole day was enjoyable, and it even smelt like Christmas. We played charades, hide and seek and with the train set. We ate a lunch of what seemed like an enormous amount of food. The afternoon was spent walking in the park where Vera and Angus looked so happy and relaxed, pushing Olive in her Silver Cross pram. The boys had brought bread with them, to feed the ducks, who behaved as though they had not been fed in weeks. Alfie was so enthusiastic with his bread throwing that I had to work hard to stop him from falling into the water.

On Boxing Day, Angus's brother Ian, his wife Dora and their two sons, Seth and Edwin came to visit. The boys were older than John and Alfie, but they seemed happy to play football with them in the park. Dora looked very glamorous wearing a cream mid-calf length dress, which was the utmost in the latest fashion. The dress had slightly flared panel inserts and bell cuffs on three quarter length sleeves. It fitted her slim figure beautifully and I could see that the cut of the fabric was superb. I complimented her on her dress, and she went to great lengths to tell me that it was from a London designer, the implication being I suppose, that it was expensive.

Dora directed my attention to her stunning jewellery as being, real diamonds and very Art Deco. I quickly gathered that she considered herself to be sophisticated as she smoked black cigarettes, using a long mother of pearl holder. Her conversation with me was limited to telling me that Ian was a successful barrister and a KC, which Vera later told me stood for Kings Counsel.

Angus and Ian spent most of the afternoon in the study, deep in conversation. Angus looked worried most of the day and I gathered that it was to do with work.

The great depression had affected all the workplaces in the country, including Landsdown Short iron and steel works, where he was Managing Director and so had a great deal of responsibility.

The company, which was the main employer in the town and further afield into the next county, was famous for the huge bridges it constructed worldwide. To me it seemed a shame that Angus should have to be worried about work on Boxing Day, but I had the feeling that he found talking to his brother helpful.

By the New Year we had started to think about the boys going back to Groat Cottage. Vera had written a letter to Herbert Flitch offering for Angus to take them home, in readiness for John starting his new school term. Needless to say, there had not been a reply and it was now the second week in January 1932.

The front doorbell rang, and I opened it to find Mrs Flitch standing there with her usual frosty face which I'm sure she saved just for me.

"Oh! It's you Betty Dawson, well I want to see the organ grinder not the monkey. Is Vera in?" Mrs Flitch said.

I did not like the woman, but I invited her in, and asked her, politely, to wait in the hall.

I thought as I looked at her, 'Charm and charisma has passed that one by.'

"It's my Herby," Flitch the witch said. "He's bad with his nerves and there's no way we can have the boys back, I just could not cope. And by the way Betty

Dawson, I know that you stole that medal which rightfully belongs to my son, as he was next of kin to your mother. What's more, I intend to get it back."

Before I could respond Vera joined us in the hall and I noticed that Mrs Flitch's whole demeanour changed, especially when she was offered refreshments.

Vera said, "Bettina, would you please take Mrs Flitch into the morning room and I will go and ask Mrs Handyside to bring us some tea."

Over tea, sandwiches, cake and scones with cream and jam, Mrs Flitch admired the china tea service and the lovely linen napkins, but she did not ask after any of the children. She just kept repeating that neither she nor Herbert were well enough to have the boys at Little Laxlet, whilst eating a hearty afternoon tea.

'Not much wrong with her appetite,' I thought.

Vera said, "Well I'll have to talk to Angus about a more permanent arrangement for John and Alfie, but if they do stay with us longer, then John will need to go to school."

Mrs Flitch replied, "If you can't have them then the only other option is the welfare. They can take them. I'm adamant, I just cannot cope, what with my legs and Herby's bad nerves."

I did wonder that if Maisie's boyfriend was still around, he might be the cause of Herbert's bad nerves!

"I'm off then, I have shopping to do and a train to catch," said Mrs Flitch, putting an envelope on the table.

"You'll find their birth certificates in there. If the boys can't stay with you just send them back, their birth certificates with them," she went on.

As she left her parting shot was, "I'll need to know by next week because if you do not want them then I'll get in touch with the council."

She spoke about her grandchildren as if they were nothing to her. Vera and I both stood at the door, stunned and mortified at her lack of caring.

As Flitch the Witch 'flew' down the path, I imagined her hat becoming pointed and I thought to myself, 'train? — broomstick more like.'

Vera was born to be a mother and she loved baby Olive unconditionally. Although she cared for John and Alfie, she hadn't bargained on them staying for longer than the Christmas holidays. Mrs Flitch had threatened to put them into care and as far as we could see, she meant it.

Angus and Vera were the kindest people I have ever met, and the boys stayed on at Iona House. By the end of January, John was enrolled in school and I took him every morning and collected him every afternoon, with Alfie walking with us. If the boys were staying indefinitely then Alfie would be attending the same school in September.

January 1932 was wet which meant that we all had to wear wellingtons and waterproof capes. I always seemed to have rainwater dripping off my nose and trickling down my back. I often thought that if only it would only snow, then sledging to school would be much more fun than trudging through the rain.

Mrs Scribbins was now struggling on her own with all the extra washing that the sudden increase in family numbers had created. The copper boiler warmed the wash house, but the rinsing water was freezing. Possing the sudsy wash in the zinc tub was heavy work and it cannot have been much fun, although Mrs Scribbins was always very cheerful. Sometimes I would help with the sorting of the clothes and then turning the big mangle, as she fed the rinsed clothes through.

Sucking in her breath she would say, "Me 'ands is red raw Miss Bettina, I'll not 'arf be glad when it's summer."

In the warmth of the kitchen, we would hang the wet clothes on the pulley to dry and then pull it up, hoping that the ropes would not break. Mrs Scribbins would then have her tea and 'snap', as she called it, rubbing salve into her red hands to ease the soreness. In conversation I had told her that I liked doing crosswords as did Uncle Angus. She was very impressed, and told me she could hardly read and write herself.

"Not 'aving 'ad a proper heducation like," she said.

She then said, "The 'arrisons get the Hexpress every day and I use it to start the fire in their kitchen range. I don't think they do the crossword. Shall I cut it out and keep it for you?"

"That would be very kind of you Mrs Scribbins," I replied.

As the household had grown so rapidly Vera arranged for the bedlinen and towels to be collected and taken weekly to the laundry. Mrs Scribbins was not at all happy about this, fearing a loss of income when work was hard to find.

However, Vera asked her, "Would you like to come in on a Tuesday and iron for us?"

To which Mrs Scribbins readily agreed. I could see she was thinking that a job in a warm kitchen would be very acceptable indeed.

In February 1932 Vera and Angus went to the court to finalise the adoption of baby Olive. On returning home, they were ecstatically happy when they showed me the new adoption certificate for their daughter now named, Claudette Olivia McLeod. My baby sister now had the name that her birth mother had wanted for her. Claudette Olivia just sat in her pram, smiling and showing her two new bottom teeth, oblivious as to why we were all so happy and excited.

My thoughts kept returning to how I was to earn a living.

The following day I said to Vera, "It's time I had work, but I don't feel I have any skills."

"Bettina you are excellent around the home," Vera said, "I do not know how I'd manage without you."

"That's very kind," I replied, "but I really think that I should find work outside the home then I can pay my way and still help you as well."

What I really meant, but I didn't like to say, was that I would then be able to save up for a sewing machine.

That night, while I soaked in the bath, scented with Yardley's lavender bath salts, my mind drifted back to Groat Cottage when it was just Mam and me. Our tin bath hung on a hook on the yard wall and on Friday nights we would fill it with hot water from the side boiler which was part of the range fire. First, I would have my hair washed then into the tin bath for a good wash, with Imperial Leather soap. Louisa would have a towel and my nightdress warming by the fire; it was so cosy and lovely having a bath in our sitting room. After I had gone to bed, she would add some more hot water to the bath, immerse herself and relax.

The following morning the bath water would be used to scrub the front doorstep, then it would be used to swill down the path in front of the Groat Cottage before she started her cleaning job at the pub.

It was never the same once Herbert Flitch moved in with us. My mother always made sure that he was at the pub or out with that no-good Dickie Pearson on our bath nights.

CHAPTER 9

Visitors

Planning and preparing for Easter was great fun at Iona House; the gardens were really pretty and ideal for an Easter Egg hunt. We boiled eggs in onion skins to marble them and the boys painted theirs. Egg jarping, which is a serious northern custom, took place on Good Friday when we had hot cross buns and hard-boiled eggs for breakfast.

Mrs Handyside sang her husband's praises constantly but I had to acknowledge that the show of spring flowers in the garden was glorious. Vera always enjoyed having a vase of fresh flowers in the hall and when I returned home from taking John and Alfie to the park, the perfume of narcissus filled the air, which I found both uplifting and comforting.

Vera greeted me with, "I'm going to learn to drive the Ford."

This surprised me somewhat as she had always said that it wasn't necessary to drive as the town was so accessible.

"It's going to be fantastic driving the children out into the country for summer picnics," she added.

Now as much as I love my Auntie Vera, the thought of her driving a car filled me with trepidation. Pushing the big Silver Cross pram had pedestrians fearing for their lives, as she seemed oblivious to anyone else on the pavement.

Angus was chauffeured by Percy, (the chauffeur and/or handyman) in the Bentley mostly these days although sometimes he drove it himself.

"I already have a license and this afternoon Angus is coming home early to take me for a run out in the Ford," Vera said.

I caught the look in Mrs Handyside's eye and her raised eyebrow which gave me the distinct impression that she feared the same as I did, regarding Vera and driving.

My role in the household was one that I felt I had slipped into, that of caring for the boys and generally helping Vera, Mrs Handyside and Mrs Scribbins. Although I did enjoy being a part of what made the house run smoothly and Vera gave me pocket money, I was not addressing the challenge of my not having a job, which I found frustrating at times.

Claudette was an exceptionally contented baby and it was fun taking her and Alfie to the park most afternoons. We would see the nannies in their smart brown uniforms looking after their charges. The children with the nannies were not allowed to mix with any other children, unless also accompanied by a nanny.

As for the nannies themselves, I found them rather cliquey.

If I ever tried to be polite by saying, "Good afternoon," I was ignored and I soon realised that they only spoke to one another.

However, I did hear some unusual snippets of their conversations such as not being allowed to go to Woolworths on their days off, in case they brought germs home, food being rationed in the households and not being allowed time off, which was due to them.

Another nanny was complaining one day about the father in her placement who wouldn't keep his hands to himself and that she was looking for another family. I do believe I overheard her use the term 'groping bastard', so I quickly moved on so that Alfie would not hear.

We always took bread to feed the ducks and Alfie enjoyed being pushed on the swings. Even though I enjoyed our outings to the park I felt lonely and missed having someone my own age to talk to.

Instead, I eavesdropped on the nannies and I thought to myself, 'How sad is that.' I then gave myself a good talking to in the style of, 'You don't know how lucky you are, Bettina Dawson, get over yourself.'

True to his word, Angus had come home early to take Vera for a driving lesson. He had anticipated finding a quiet road for her first experience at the wheel and he had even identified such a road. Not so for Vera who thought that driving aimlessly about, as she put it, would be a waste of time; to go to the market would be a much better idea.

They were not gone long.

I had never witnessed them ever having a cross word before, but they returned, shouting at each other and slamming doors. Vera was in a fury and she stormed straight upstairs, while Angus muttered something under his breath about grinding and ruining the gears.

Angus said, "Your Auntie Vera has just demolished a stall full of hardware down at the market. There were pots and pans all over the place and the stall holder had to jump for his life. It has cost me a pretty penny I can tell you."

Although he looked rather cross, I thought that he seemed quite calm, considering!

I said, "Well as long as no one was hurt."

Angus said, "No, no one was hurt but the car has a huge dent in it now."

He then went into his study where he remained for some time.

From then on, Percy was in charge of Vera's driving instruction. He was a very patient teacher, but always looked incredibly pale with clenched fists when they returned home. I also noticed that following a driving lesson his hand shook a little as he drank his tea.

It was not long before Vera announced that she was fully proficient, competent and safe to drive. She had heard that before too long a driving test would be introduced, which would be compulsory.

She said, "It's just marvellous that I'm such a natural driver and I won't be required to take such a test!"

I was hanging out the washing with Mrs Scribbins one morning when Stan Handyside asked me, "Could I have a private word Bettina?"

At this Mrs Scribbins ears pricked up, so Stan and I walked down the garden out of her earshot. He looked very shy and kept shuffling his feet.

He said, "Can I take you to the pictures?"

I did not quite know what to say, so replied, "Yes, but I'll have to ask Auntie Vera first."

The film was Tarzan the Ape Man and it was on at the 'Roxy'.

Stan was seventeen years old and very quiet and respectful. On most days he helped his father with the Iona House gardens but he did have other gardening jobs elsewhere.

Vera said, "Yes you can go, if Uncle Angus agrees but he will need to have a word with Stan first."

Poor Stan looked very nervous as he entered Angus's study with its huge, polished mahogany desk and walls lined with important looking books. I was later told, by Stan, that Angus had given him a stern warning about how to behave with a young lady and to bring me home safely.

The thought of a night out at the pictures was very exciting for me. I had never been before, however I did feel sorry for Stan having to receive a grilling from Angus.

Stan called for me and we walked to the 'Roxy', where he insisted on paying for the seats which were 3d each and he even bought a bar of chocolate from a machine for us to share. I thought that he looked very smart in his best tweed jacket and flat cap, quite different from when he was gardening with his dad when they both wore blue overalls.

I enjoyed the Pathé News and hearing Ramsay MacDonald, the Prime Minister speaking. 'Tarzan The Ape Man' was an enjoyable film and my first experience of seeing the jungle and a man swinging through the trees.

As we walked back to Iona House the conversation was mostly about Stan's pigeons which did not hold great interest for me. Other than that, I think we were both a bit shy and tongue tied so, at the door, I quickly thanked Stan for a lovely evening, and went indoors. He looked a bit sad as he walked away — perhaps he had hoped for a goodnight kiss.

I had noticed a curtain twitch and suspected that Vera was peeping out, waiting for my return.

The next day Mrs Scribbins was very anxious to hear about 'the date' as she called it.

"Did he kiss you on the lips?" she asked.

She seemed disappointed at my reply.

"Our Mabel's in the family way again," Mrs Scribbins said. Mabel was her only daughter and not much older than me. "Will she never learn." She went on, "'er lad told 'er you can't fall if you do it standing up and she told me they 'ad never 'done it' except standing up and this was the second time."

Mabel was unmarried and could not be very bright to have fallen for that line a second time, I thought.

Mrs Scribbins then said, "Never heven been to bed together, 'anky-panky in me little back end and 'e's disappeared into thin air."

I later discovered that Mrs Scribbins' little back end' was the tiny porch attached to her tenement flat.

"Cousin Crispin is coming to stay," Vera announced. "There is to be a tennis tournament in the park, and he is an ace player."

Crispin was Angus's young cousin and a student of Classics and Divinity at Oxford University. 'Up at Oxford' they called it which was hard to understand as Oxford is south of Ransington.

He made quite an entrance in his red MG sports car. Several tennis racquets poked out from behind the rear seat. I thought he looked okay but not handsome. However, he did have a wonderful, wild mass of black curly hair which was held in place with a bright red bandeau around his head, stopping it from blowing into his eyes. He wore sports slacks with a matching top, a tennis sweater and a cravat which gave me the impression that he fancied himself as being suave and sophisticated.

Mrs Handyside had warned me, with trepidation in her voice, that the house would be in turmoil for the duration of his stay. 'The chinless wonder,' as she called him, had stayed at Iona House before so she had experienced it, and by the look on her face, not a good one.

For a man of twenty years old Crispin was useless and immature. Yes, he was good at tennis and no doubt good at his studies but having said that I've said it all. He left a trail of his stuff all over the house, never as much as removed a plate from the table and as for the toilet he used, it quickly became a 'no-go-zone' for me. When he was over at the park playing tennis, we all breathed a sigh of relief.

I took a telephone message from a lady called Minky to say that she would be arriving at four p.m. and that she required to be collected from the railway station.

'Poor Minky', as she was referred to, was a spinster, her fiancé having been killed fighting in the war in 1917.

Vera was visibly in a flap as Minky was not expected for three weeks.

"The only guest room with a bed made up is the big room next to you Bettina," she said.

Percy was asked to go to the railway station to meet Minky whilst Vera and I checked the room and put out clean towels and a pretty vase of flowers to welcome the guest.

Maiden aunts and cousins, and there were many of them in the 1930s, spent a lot of their time frequenting the homes of their relatives as a means of,

a) easing their loneliness

b) eking out their income

In other words, a free holiday.

'Poor Minky' arrived and she was quite a revelation to me as she looked anything but poor. She wore the latest chic fashion, had dyed blond hair with, I suspect a Marcel wave; bright red lips with matching fingernails and mascara filled her eyelashes. Her stockings were silk and expensive looking, but I did notice that her scent was cheap. I overheard a comment from Mrs Handyside to Mrs Scribbins where the phrase 'sugar daddy' was mentioned!

I took 'Poor Minky' up to her room which was indeed next to mine with Crispin's room further along the landing.

The attraction between Minky and Crispin was instantaneous and electric even though she was at least twenty years older than him.

The squeaky floorboards on the landing told me that a session of hot passion was imminent in the room next door, most nights and even some afternoons. Minky would retire with a 'headache' followed by Crispin who needed to 'rest' before or after a tennis match.

Now I do understand sex and procreation, having lived in the country all my life, but their sexual adventures were on a different level. Ravenous with lust, Minky enjoyed very noisy sex as apparently, equally as ravenous, did Crispin, both shouting expletives such as 'yes, yes', 'get it in big boy', 'that's wonderful', 'great', 'fantastic', 'more, more', all at the top of their voices. I did begin to wonder if one of them suffered from hearing loss, so loud was their shouting.

I always knew when their lively sex session was about to conclude as Crispin would shout, 'Jeronimo' and I would think 'Thank God for that. Perhaps now I can get some sleep.' There was much groaning, moaning, laughing and even cheering during Crispin and Minky's two week stay that they really, and I do mean really, tested the bedsprings.

Fortunately, the children slept through all the noise and Vera and Angus made no comment.

Having relatives to stay at Iona House was, apparently, quite the norm but we were all very happy to wave 'Poor Minky' and Crispin on their way — if only to get an undisturbed night's sleep.

Mrs Handyside and I went into, what was considered, the best guest room, to change the sheets, ready for the laundry after Minky had left. Vera called it 'The Blue Room' with its beautiful blue and white handmade quilt which was her pride and joy. The room overlooked the park and hanging from the ceiling was a gorgeous huge crystal chandelier which Angus and Vera had brought back from Italy where they had spent their honeymoon.

Opening the curtains, we saw the terrible state of the room which shocked and horrified us. The malodorous smell of Minky's cheap scent, combined with sweat and nicotine was overpowering.

Mrs Handyside said, "Bettina please would you go and find Mrs Scribbins for me. This room is not fit for a young girl's eyes to see?"

When I asked her, Mrs Scribbins came running straight away, eager to see the state of the room.

"Well I'm glad I'm not washing those sheets, the dirty buggers," she said.

There were empty champagne bottles under the bed with empty glasses, two ashtrays brimming with cigarette butts and several empty beer bottles. Vera's beautiful embroidered pillowcases were covered in lipstick, foundation and black mascara. The lovely blue and white quilt was just thrown in a corner with a huge wine stain on it. Worst of all, a pair of Crispin's, not very clean, underpants were lodged up in the chandelier.

Crispin and Minky had a passionate liking for rough, raucous sex and he would kick his underpants up in the air, aiming for the chandelier. If they landed on the target, they would both give a cheer. He also liked to be tied to the headboard with the belt from her silk dressing gown she would then tease him, intimately, with a riding crop.

When the two women found the riding crop it was then that they realised the extent of Crispin and Minky's kinkiness and they started to laugh.

"And him going to be a vicar," Mrs Handyside said.

"A vicar! Some vicar 'e'll be," said Mrs Scribbins. "Well, all I can say is then 'eaven 'elp 'is fucking flock."

At this they were both laughing uncontrollably and when I left them, sitting together on the blanket chest, the tears were rolling down their faces, which they blotted away with their floral pinnies.

CHAPTER 10

A Day Out

The blue and white quilt from the best guest room was washed on a sunny summers day and Mrs Scribbins and I hung it on the washing line. It dried perfectly in a gentle warm breeze.

Knowing how much I had admired the quilt Vera said, "How would you enjoy a day meeting some of the ladies who make the quilts?"

Unsure as to where the quilters lived, I asked if she would be going with me and she assured me that we would go as a family.

John was having his summer holiday from school so, although I knew that I would enjoy the trip out, I was not sure if it was the kind of day out the boys would look forward to and I expressed this to Vera.

She said, "It won't be a problem as several of the quilting ladies have children, so there will be playmates for John and Alfie."

The quilters were the wives of Durham miners living in a pit village, so the journey would take about an hour each way.

"My plan," Vera said, "is to take the Ford."

I felt very unsure about such a long journey with Vera at the wheel.

When Angus came home that evening Vera told him of her plan.

He said, "That is fine, you will enjoy a day out but I'm not keen on you driving such a long way. You haven't been driving long enough."

The tone of his voice was firm, and it was clear to me that Vera would not be driving up into County Durham.

She did not protest, which was unusual as Vera liked, and was accustomed to, having her own way.

"Percy will take you all in the Bentley and I will drive myself to the works in the Ford," Angus said.

Vera looked rather coy and I wondered if that was her plan all along.

On our journey to County Durham, Vera told me, "The women make and sell the quilts to raise funds for the miners' welfare scheme."

Vera supported the scheme and she donated two raffle prizes of an elegant ladies' silk scarf and a pair of men's leather gloves for the miners' summer fete and sports day, which was to take place soon.

Claudette slept for most of the journey and the boys enjoyed travelling in such a big car, seeing the day out as a big adventure.

Six quilting ladies worked in the tiny front room of one of the miners' cottages very close to the pit. I was amazed at how clean and neat the cottage was, having seen so much coal dust covering everything outside.

I was mesmerised to see how they worked on the quilt which was held and supported in a big wooden frame, which practically filled the room, with barely enough space for their chairs. They explained to me how the quilt was made up of three layers with cotton fabric on either side of a woollen blanket, like a sandwich. The more experienced quilters hand-quilted through the layers following a traditional feather pattern. Other ladies threaded needles, made cups of tea and sang gentle local folk songs with everyone joining in the chorus, then chatting to each other between the songs.

One lady called Jenny asked me, "Would you like to have a try?"

I'd been observing her closely, so was keen to try. She made me comfortable on her chair and then very quickly I was quilting, and it felt good. So good in fact that I could have kept going all day. I later realised that I had experienced an iconic moment and would love quilting forever.

Jenny drew the other ladies' attention to my quilting and they complimented me, and asked where I'd learnt to sew.

"My mother taught me," I said.

"But Vera said she can't sew," another lady said.

"Vera is not my mother, she is my Auntie, my mam died last year and now I live with Vera and Angus," I explained.

They all said they were sorry, and looked a bit embarrassed.

I said, "Look, please don't worry, you were not to know about my mother." I hoped this would make them feel better.

I quilted with them for about half an hour then I thanked them, and said, "I'd better go and see what John and Alfie are up to."

Vera was feeding Claudette stewed apple and custard whilst chatting with Mrs Ainsworth in the kitchen. She was the leader of the quilting group and she organised the days for quilting.

"Do you know where the boys are?" I asked Vera.

"Oh, don't you worry Bettina they are playing football in the lane," answered Vera and Mrs Ainsworth in unison.

They then both started laughing. I had to admit there was a very happy, cheerful atmosphere.

Sure enough, John and Alfie were in the back lane, with dustbins for goal posts, enjoying a game of football with the local boys. There was a lot of shouting and banter and I could see that they were having a good time.

The pit whistle sounded, followed by the sight of the wheel turning at the pit head denoting the end of a shift; soon, a stream of miners was coming our way. Their coal dust blackened faces looked tired as they laughed and talked with each other while trudging home. I noticed their teeth looked very white and the inside of their mouths very pink against blackened, dry lips from which came the banter of men who depended on each other for comradeship and safety in the mine. All wearing leather knee pads and heavy boots, they sounded a weary note as they marched towards us, on their way to their pit cottages.

A young woman, wearing a plain dress and a shawl came out of a back gate and she ran to meet her husband as he walked into the lane.

"Your bath is ready, and your dinner won't be long," she said to him.

"What's for dinner?" he asked her.

"Corned beef and tatty pie," was her reply.

"Good, I'm starving," he said. "It's my favourite."

"Well you're not eating 'till I wash all that coal off you," she answered laughing, smiling up at him and looking very happy.

I later discovered they were newlyweds.

Another miner on his way home said, "That lad of yours has amazing control of the ball, he could end up a professional one day. He might even play for England."

I thought that he meant John but in fact he meant Alfie.

The men stood a while watching the game, cheering when a goal was scored then they went home for a bath, food and a sleep. I could not help but think that to dig for coal in a dark, dangerous pit was not a job I would want.

The quilters stopped for a break and we had sandwiches and cake. During the break Jenny showed me some patchwork that she was working on in her spare time. The colours of the cotton fabric were vibrant and even in its unfinished state I could see Jenny was making something beautiful.

She told me, "It's called paper piecing, I'm sure you could do it."

I said, "It's lovely, I think I would love to give it a try."

Jenny said, "Here are a few hexagons to start you off with. I just cut mine out of old magazines."

She also wrote her name and address on a piece of paper and asked me to write to her if I was stuck with the paper piecing. I thanked her and popped the hexagons and her address into my bag.

Percy had been for a walk around the village where the rows of cottages looked out towards the pit and the slag heap beyond. Waste from the mine was constantly being dumped from overhead tubs onto the heap. Women, hanging out lines of washing between the cottages, all greeted Percy in a friendly way. He came upon some allotments where the miners grew flowers and vegetables for their families.

The contrast of the colourful dahlias and the delicious smell of tomatoes in the greenhouse gave Percy an insight into how important being in the light and seeing plants grow was to the miners who spent their working time in the dark. Percy struck up a conversation with a miner who had won prizes for his leeks and chrysanthemums at the annual shows and he thanked him for the tips which he could now pass on to Mr Handyside.

Vera paid for and collected two quilts which she had ordered on a previous visit. She then ordered two more quilts to collect the next time. All the quilting ladies told us how beautiful baby Claudette was whilst she smiled and babbled at her audience in a most responsive way, as she was passed around for cuddles with most of them.

As we said our goodbyes the ladies commented to me on how well-behaved John and Alfie had been and then added to bring them back next time, which pleased me as I felt that good manners and behaviour were very important.

The day spent with these hard-working women, so willing to share their knowledge with me had been memorable and now, of course I wanted to make a quilt, as well as my own clothes.

Back at Iona House I noticed a vacuum cleaner advertisement in the newspaper, and thought what a wonderful, labour saving device it must be. The task of beating the rugs on the clothesline just covered the beater, usually me, with dust. No matter how hard a beating I gave them they still seemed to be dusty.

One advertisement offered to give a free home demonstration, so I showed Mrs Handyside the paper and she said, "I like the sound of that. Do you think your Aunt Vera would agree to it?"

"There is only one way to find out and that is to ask her," I replied.

Vera thought that it was a wonderful idea and I arranged a demonstration for a few days later.

Mr Jones, who described himself as a Commercial Vacuum Cleaner Agent arrived promptly at Iona House with not one but two vacuum cleaners. Following his telephone instructions, I had prepared an area in the drawing room in readiness for his demonstration. He seemed very pleased to have an audience of Vera, myself, Mr and Mrs Handyside and Mrs Scribbins, all sitting in a semicircle awaiting, with great anticipation, to witness the magic of the vacuum cleaner.

He removed his jacket and donned a white coat as if he was a hospital doctor and asked us if we were ready for him to begin. We nodded in response.

"Then I will proceed," he said.

He then asked John and Alfie if they would be his helpers; to which they readily agreed.

"Now John," said Mr Jones, "please sprinkle those dried porridge oats onto the carpet."

This John did, taking his task very seriously.

"Now Alfie," said Mr Jones, "please sprinkle those dry tea leaves onto the carpet."

Which Alfie did, equally as seriously.

With a flourish Mr Jones switched on the upright machine and it sucked up the oats and the tea leaves, leaving the carpet impressively bright and clean.

The performance was repeated with the cylinder model and the results were just as spectacular.

We were all transfixed to have witnessed, with such speed and lack of effort, the removal of debris from the carpet.

Mrs Handyside now cleaned at Iona House three days each week and she knew that a vacuum cleaner would make her life much easier.

Mr Jones went on to demonstrate, with a further flourish, how to empty the bags, which collected the dirt and it all looked very easy.

"Which one shall we have?" Vera asked us.

We all had different ideas on which was the best, but it was Mrs Handyside who was asked to make the final decision as she was the person in charge of housekeeping, and would use it most.

"I think the cylinder model would suit us well here," she said, "as we have a huge number of stairs."

Vera ordered the cylinder model and Mr Jones was very pleased to take her order. The cost would be twelve guineas and the machine would have a two-year guarantee.

As he left, Mr Jones said, "Thank you boys for your help and thank you Mrs McLeod for your order, your machine will be with you within the week."

John and Alfie were jumping up and down with pleasure as Mr Jones had given them each a penny for helping.

Stan and I continued to go to the 'Roxy' together every few weeks, depending on which picture was showing. My favourites were musicals and Stan liked the horror films which I did not, as it meant that I had to clasp my hands over my eyes for the scary bits. We both enjoyed Charlie Chaplin films and the Pathé News, which seemed to have a lot about cricket. On the way home, we would walk slowly, sharing a bag of chips with plenty of salt and vinegar.

Stan talked a great deal about his pigeons, and I continued to make every effort to seem interested, which was difficult. I told him about my visit to the quilting ladies in County Durham and how I planned to start paper piecing with hexagons. I could not tell if Stan was interested or not but the next day, he brought me a hundred paper hexagons he had cut out from his mother's old magazines.

I realised that I felt happier than I had in a long time and that it was good to have a friend like Stan.

CHAPTER 11

September 1932

Alfie now went to school with John, but he did not settle down so well; crying that first day when I left him in the classroom, wearing his oversized uniform. He looked so little. I shed a few tears on my walk home.

Claudette had had her first birthday at the end of August and she just loved tearing open her presents whilst we all sang 'Happy Birthday' at her tea party. All babies are lovely, but as babies go, we naturally thought that she was fantastic. She could crawl now, as well as pull herself up to a stand whilst holding onto the furniture. She loved music and when we played a record on the gramophone she would bob up and down to the tune, singing along in her own baby language.

Angus had two very sturdy nursery fireguards made at the foundry and the young man who delivered them also fixed them to the wall.

"Good idea this," he said. "There's many a bairn been burnt by fire, no sense of danger at that age."

He was correct as Claudette had already investigated the hearth and its contents. Luckily, there was no fire in the grate at the time.

I was making really good progress stitching my hexagons in the morning room when Vera came in and said, "Claudette is having her nap but I wonder if you could listen for her as I have to pop out for about half an hour, or I may be slightly longer, but certainly no more than an hour."

I replied, "Yes of course I will, but what time is our visitor due to arrive?"

Vera had previously told me that her aunt, who was my great aunt, was coming to stay at Iona House, as she did every year. No one knew for how long, as aunt Eliza Jane never gave time periods, but it was usually for about a week.

"Oh," Vera said, "no need to worry, Percy is going to collect her from her home in Newcastle as she is now a good age and I don't want her travelling by herself on a train. I think they should be here at about five p.m."

I relaxed as I knew the guest room was ready for aunt Eliza Jane, which meant I would have the luxury of an hour or so for stitching, whilst Claudette had her nap.

Vera was about to leave when she hesitated. She then closed the door as Mrs Handyside was in the next room.

"I'm going to see Dr Salmanowicz about a rather personal problem which has been troubling me for a while,"

She now had my full attention, as Mam's death had hit me hard and I certainly did not want anything bad to happen to Vera.

Vera was six feet tall and astonishingly elegant but when I looked at her more closely, I could see that this strong woman was showing signs of tiredness and worry.

"I hadn't realised you were feeling unwell," I said. "I know that you had some broken nights with Claudette due to her teething, but does Uncle Angus know?"

"No, and I do not want him to," Vera said, with panic in her face. "Angus would whisk me off to some specialist and then we would both be worried. He has enough on his plate at the moment, over at the Works, so I do not want to add to it."

"Perhaps Dr Salmanowicz will give you a tonic. You look pale and tired. Do you think you could be anaemic?" I said.

"Who knows," she replied. "But I really must see him today, my haemorrhoids are so bad I can hardly sit down."

Poor Vera, I thought as she left, what she could do with is a holiday not a visitor coming to stay. I then remembered a Daily Express crossword which Mrs Scribbins had brought me the previous day, so I did that to help stop my mind from working overtime and worrying about Vera and her illness.

Mrs Handyside put her head round the door to say that Claudette was awake, and would I like a cup of tea.

I knew that she would be wondering where Vera had gone but I decided not to tell her as it was private.

Vera returned an hour later; she didn't say a word, she just sat in a chair staring ahead for what seemed an eternity.

It must be really bad news, I feared.

She looked dazed but eventually said, "Bettina, please will you telephone uncle Angus at his office and ask him to come home as soon as he can?"

It must be news of the worst kind I thought because I'd never known Vera to ask for Angus to come home in the day before. I did as she asked. I then took her a cup of tea and we waited for Angus to arrive.

As Angus walked in the door Vera burst into tears and she blurted out, "I'm expecting a baby. Dr Salmanowicz just told me."

The look of disbelief on Angus's face was astounding and he then asked the questions.

"I can't believe it. When is the baby due? Is Dr Salmanowicz absolutely sure? Shouldn't you have some sort of pregnancy test?"

"About a month from now," Vera replied. "I just thought that I might be having an early change of life."

As for me, I didn't know whether to laugh or cry, I was so delighted that Vera didn't have some awful illness.

Dr Salmanowicz had told Vera that it was rare and unusual, although not unheard of, for some women to be pregnant and not realise that they were until some months had passed.

Angus then took charge and said, "We will need a fully equipped nursery and a maternity nurse which will all be arranged before the baby is born. I will contact Mr Sturgis, the Obstetrician, you will be under his care Vera and he will recommend a nurse."

I could see that the shock had put his brain into overdrive.

Vera smiled and said, "Angus, the baby is not due for at least another month and I really do not think that we will need a maternity nurse."

"But you will agree to see the specialist won't you, for reassurance, that is all I ask. I need you to have the best possible care and to know that all is well."

Vera just nodded.

Angus then said, "Good, then I will arrange an appointment for you tomorrow if possible."

Vera asked me to bring Mrs Handyside into the drawing room to give her the news. I had an idea that Mrs Handyside already knew as, when I opened the door into the hall, she was dusting, very diligently, just the other side!

Percy arrived with aunt Eliza Jane at five p.m. as predicted. Their journey from Newcastle had been straightforward although Percy told us that he found aunt's habit of waving, in a Royal manner, to pedestrians to be rather disconcerting. Eliza Jane was a great royalist and she particularly admired Queen Mary and even wore several strands of pearls and similar hats to the Queen.

Eliza Jane and my Grandmother, Letitia Ann, had been sisters and as children they had had a very comfortable life in a grand house in the country, near their father's mine. They did not go to school, but they had a governess, a piano tutor and were taught sewing and embroidery. Sadly, their father died when they were quite young and the mine was sold, which is when they moved to Newcastle-upon-Tyne, where their mother bought a big house, took in boarders, mostly acts from the music hall, and made a good living.

"Well Bettina I haven't seen you for many a long year," Eliza Jane said. giving me a big hug, "You look just like Louisa. How are you pet?"

I answered, "Very well thank you great aunt. I hope you are not too tired after your journey; would you like to have a little rest before dinner?"

"No thank you Bettina, a ride in a Bentley is like travelling on air. I might be seventy-six," she went on, "but a cup of hot, strong tea will set me just right."

I immediately liked my great aunt and I had a feeling that her visit would be an interesting one.

At dinner Vera and Angus disclosed the news of the baby to Eliza Jane and that an appointment had been made to see Mr Sturgis the following day.

I noticed Vera did not seem very hungry and after dinner she said, "Bettina, please would you bath Claudette and put her to bed for me tonight. It's been quite a day and I'm feeling so tired that I could sleep on a clothesline."

Angus, on the other hand, was grinning like a Cheshire cat, he was so pleased.

As Vera went to bed she said, "I'll be pleased to lie down, my back is aching like you wouldn't believe."

Louisa used to suffer from backache when she was pregnant, so I didn't think much of it at the time as I had a busy evening ahead. I bathed Claudette and put her in her cot in the corner of Vera and Angus's bedroom, trying not to wake Vera who was sound asleep. There had been much discussion recently regarding Claudette moving into a bedroom of her own, but Vera resisted the idea as she liked to have her near.

I bathed the boys and read them a story. John had brought a book home from school which I said he could read quietly. Alfie was already asleep. I asked John not to make any noise as we did not want to disturb auntie Vera as she was very tired.

When I went downstairs again Eliza Jane was just finishing washing and drying the dishes and Angus was catching up with some work in his study and I suspected telephoning a few people with the news.

I filled a hot water bottle for my great aunt, and made sure that she had everything she needed for the night.

Knowing how hectic mornings were at Iona House I felt it was my responsibility to make sure that the boys had a good breakfast and to get them to school on time.

Setting the table for breakfast the night before had become a habit as had polishing the boys' shoes. Whilst doing this I couldn't help thinking how much I liked Eliza Jane, who had told me that we had met before when I was very young, but I couldn't remember it.

It was about eleven p.m. when I knocked and then popped my head around the study door to say goodnight to Angus.

"Good night Bettina. It's been quite a day," he said.

I had not been in bed long when I heard the floorboards creaking on the landing and the toilet being flushed several times. I went out of my room and found Vera pacing up and down.

"The backache is unbearable," she said, "and now the pain is around the front."

She was hanging onto the banister.

She's in labour, I thought.

"Keep calm," I said to myself, not feeling at all calm

I helped Vera back to her bed, and said, "Lie on your bed Auntie, I'll get Angus, I'll only be two minutes."

I raced down the stairs and barged into the study.

"The baby is coming Uncle Angus, phone Dr Salmanowicz, straight away, quickly, his number is on the pad by the phone."

I then ran back upstairs two at a time, collecting towels from the linen cupboard on the landing as I passed it. Vera was clearly in pain and labour seemed to be progressing very fast.

She said she had a feeling of wanting to push. I said to blow out through her mouth, and showed her how, but she had a very strong urge to bear down.

Ten minutes later, a small baby boy was born into the towel I was holding; I wiped his nose and mouth, and wrapped the towel round him to keep him warm until the doctor arrived, which he did a few minutes later. Even though the baby was moving and crying I was relieved when Dr Salmanowicz walked into the bedroom. He washed his hands and cut the umbilical cord, then he handed me the baby.

"Well my dear Mrs Mcleod I did not expect to see you again quite so soon," he said. "You have a son and by the sound of his lungs he is fine."

I gently wiped some of the thick waxy vernix from the baby's head and he became quiet. I thought he looked perfect with big eyes the colour of iolite, in his tiny face. He gazed back at me for a moment, then he opened his mouth and began to cry again. He was weighed in a nappy hanging from a fisherman's weighing scale and four pounds eleven and a half ounces was recorded by Dr Salmanowicz whilst we waited for the afterbirth to be expelled; after which Angus came into the bedroom to see his wife and his new-born son.

This was the moment they had both longed for, so I left them holding and gazing at the baby who had taken everyone by surprise; this was a time just for them to share.

Quite a day, Angus had said.

Quite a night as well, I thought. Baby Claudette Olivia had slept soundly, in the same room, throughout the birth of her baby brother.

CHAPTER 12

The Nurse

The following morning at ten a.m. precisely I opened the front door to a nurse wearing a long navy-blue cape, navy blue hat and carrying a nurse's bag in her gloved hand.

"I am Maternity Nurse Milner," she said. "I'm part of Mr Sturgis's private obstetric consultancy team. I have been asked personally by Mr Sturgis, at the request of Mr McLeod, to look after Mrs McLeod and their new-born infant." Her mouth smiled but her eyes did not.

I was about to invite her in, but she walked straight past me into the hall; rather rudely, I thought. She unbuttoned her cape, took off her gloves and hat and handed them all to me, at the same time whipping a list from her uniform pocket, which was also for me.

"This is my requirements' list. Mrs McLeod will be having at least three full days of bed rest, which means that I am now responsible for her personal hygiene. There are also some things on the list which I will require for the baby. The chemist in the town stocks them all, you will get them there. Now I would like you to take me to my patient and do you have a bedpan in the house, if not, add it to the list."

It had been a hectic morning at Iona House. Aunt Eliza Jane said she had heard a new baby cry in the night but then thought that she must be dreaming, and the bed was so warm and cosy that she soon drifted back to sleep. She had helped with the breakfast for Angus, John and Alfie and I had taken Vera porridge, tea and toast on a tray about seven-thirty a.m.

Vera looked tired but happy. New baby, Rory Donald McLeod, had already had several breast feeds and he was asleep in the wicker basket beside her. Claudette was in bed with Vera happily playing 'Incy Wincy Spider climbing up the spout' and was a tad reluctant to come downstairs for her breakfast, however she hardly noticed that she had a baby brother.

Nurse Milner made it quite clear to me, by the tone in her voice and her rather officious demeanour, that she was now in charge and when I took her to Vera's bedroom she went in, closing the door firmly in my face.

Vera later told me, that the nurse had produced a schedule from her bag, regarding feeding the baby, rest times and food requirements for 'mother'. Vera was told that she must not get out of bed for at least three days, but more likely five and was to inform Nurse Milner if a bed pan was required. There would be twice daily vulval swabbing and two hours each afternoon 'mother' would spend lying on her front, to reduce the risk of prolapse.

Vera was then told, in no uncertain way.

"Baby must be in a routine before I leave you one month from now. He will be with me, in my room at night, to afford you a restful sleep and it is not good for your older child to spend too much time with you, Mrs McLeod. Perhaps one hour each day is probably enough, or you will become overtired."

Vera could impersonate Nurse Milner and the voice she used when telling me this sounded exactly like her when this appalling regime was relayed back to me.

Nurse Milner wore, over her ankle-length navy-blue dress, a spectacularly white stiffly starched apron, which had several impressive looking nurses' badges pinned to its bib, covering her rather scraggy chest. A frilly white hat, secured by hair grips, balanced on top of her bun and greasy, scraped back hair.

She sniffed, obviously unimpressed, when I showed her the bedroom which would be hers for her stay, then stated that she would take all her meals in her room and did not expect to share a bathroom.

"Here is my napkin and napkin ring, they are to go on my tray," she informed me.

I felt myself becoming annoyed at her rude, unpleasant manner but said nothing as I did not want to upset Vera.

Aunt Eliza Jane kept busy in the kitchen which was wonderful as she was a very good cook.

"And who does she think is going to take her meals up on a tray?" Eliza Jane asked when I told her that

Nurse Milner wanted to eat in her room — Certainly not you Bettina, you have enough to do," she went on.

"What do you think Edna?" she said to Mrs Handyside.

"I agree Eliza, the woman will have Bettina run off her feet if we let her. I'll tell 'Nurse starchy knickers' when lunch is ready and she can just get herself down here for it," Mrs Handyside said putting the napkin ring on the kitchen table.

I took Vera's lunch up to her on a tray and apparently there had already been a disagreement between nurse and patient.

"Why would I need a bedpan when the toilet is just next door and there is a bidet in the bathroom. As for feeding my baby by the clock that is a no, no", Vera continued, "Also there is no way my baby will be sleeping anywhere but with me."

I could see that Vera was upset. Nurse Milner had only been in the house for two hours and it was not going well.

When asked to do so by Mrs Handyside, Nurse Milner did come down to the kitchen for lunch, which was delicious soup and fresh bread, both made by Eliza Jane.

The kitchen was warm, and smelt of newly baked bread, but the atmosphere was brittle.

The napkin, which was on Nurse Milner's side plate, was removed from its ring by her. She then shook it out in what I considered to be a very snappy manner.

Eliza Jane made several attempts at conversation but Nurse Milner preferred silence, eating her food then leaving, without even saying thank you.

'It's going to be a very long month,' I thought.

Dr Salmanowicz called later in the afternoon to examine Vera and the baby and he declared all to be well. As Rory was a premature baby, he would call daily for the next ten days he told Vera, which was reassuring.

It was at this point that Nurse Milner asked to speak with Dr Salmanowicz privately outside the bedroom.

She informed him who she was and that she was, as part of Mr Sturgis's team, in charge and she required his support of her authority as Mrs McLeod was being uncooperative. Brusque words were exchanged, and I gathered from what I overheard that Dr Salmanowicz held no value concerning her regimes.

Nurse Milner then asked if she might use the telephone. She seemed unhappy about something that the doctor had said to her. She telephoned Mr Sturgis, to complain about Dr Salmanowicz and about the conditions she was expected to 'put up with' at Iona House.

Vera happened to be on the landing on her way to the bathroom and she overheard the telephone conversation taking place in the hall below which really annoyed her.

About an hour later Vera had a robust and frank discussion with Nurse Milner and she told her that, although she valued and respected her experience and qualifications, her services would be better spent on a mother who was more appreciative of her ideas and a household which could better accommodate her needs.

Nurse Milner left Iona House before five p.m., so although Uncle Angus had booked and arranged the maternity nurse, he did not even get to meet her.

Baby Rory Donald stole everyone's hearts as he was so adorable. In the early days he did have a touch of jaundice, but Vera was reassured by Dr Salmanowicz that if the baby was feeding well, he would be fine.

"That boy has the best set of lungs in the county," Eliza Jane would say. "We all know when it's his dinner time." A cuddle was something that they both enjoyed and baby Rory could often be seen being cradled on her lap.

We did wonder how Claudette would take to seeing Vera breast feeding the baby as she was a curious child and demanding of her mother's time, especially when Vera had to attend to Rory. Vera's solution to keep her daughter close and out of mischief when she was feeding was to offer Claudette the other breast. This had novelty value for this bright little girl at first, but she soon began to enjoy the warm, sweet milk so, problem solved. Vera was sublimely happy feeding both her babies at the same time, supported with big feather cushions and stroking their beautiful silky heads.

Life at Iona House seemed busier than ever and Vera was happy for Eliza Jane to be in charge of the kitchen.

"Is there any chance that man of yours could come by a couple of rabbits for me Edna?" she asked Mrs Handyside. "If he can then I'll make a rabbit pie for Saturday tea and I'll do one for you as well."

"I'll ask him," Mrs Handyside replied, "and if there's a pie in it for us I can guarantee he'll find you a couple of rabbits."

Eliza Jane was a legend in the family regarding her rabbit pies which were delicious, topped with 'melt in the mouth' crisp, golden pastry. This would be a tea for everyone to look forward to and enjoy.

Most days Eliza Jane and I managed to sit together and relax for an hour in the morning room. I would sew my hexagons, which Jenny had told me was 'Grandmothers Garden' pattern, while she worked her way through the mending. There were always buttons to sew on, rips to mend, holes to patch and socks to darn. To watch her darn a sock over a wooden mushroom, was to observe an artist at work.

When she wasn't mending clothes or darning, she would be knitting socks on four needles then she would suddenly say, "Time for forty winks."

She would drop off to sleep in an instant at which point her top set of false teeth would drop to her lower jaw. The denture did not fit properly as it had been her husband's and he had only had it made a short time before he died. She told me that the denture had been expensive, and it would have been a shame to throw it out, so she had kept it until she had the need for false teeth.

However, she did have one problem which was wind. Eliza Jane passed flatus so frequently that members of the household were well used to it and accepted her 'windy moments' as the norm. Not so, visitors.

On one occasion Angus had an important guest from the Chamber of Commerce with him in the study and they were discussing, what I imagine would have been, very important matters.

My aunt and I were in the kitchen when she said, 'I just heard the front gate, it'll be the paper boy with the Gazette. I'll go and get it."

She then went from the kitchen into the hall at exactly the same time as Angus and his visitor came out of the study. Angus introduced Sir Humphrey Newman to Eliza Jane, and they shook hands.

She said, "Very pleased to meet you." In her best regal accent.

Aunt Eliza Jane then walked past them to the door mat, bent down to pick up the Gazette and farted — it was very long and very loud.

Totally unperturbed she stood up with the newspaper, pulled herself up to her full five feet, looked over the top of her wire- rimmed spectacles at Sir Humphrey and, again in her posh, regal voice said, "Never fear young man, I'm told my farts have no unpleasant smell."

Head held high, she then returned to the kitchen.

During my sewing sessions with Eliza Jane, our conversation often 'went down memory lane'. Her late husband, also John but known as Jack, had been a joiner and funeral director, a career which was highly recommended by my Great Aunt as being very secure with no shortage of customers. Her two daughters, Winnie and Gladys were both married to funeral directors. They worked in the business and had plans for expansion which seemed quite ambitious.

Aunt Eliza Jane was such a jolly person that I found it difficult to imagine her being the head of a funeral dynasty.

We talked about Louisa a great deal and she said that at home she had a framed photograph of her with dad and me. She thought I looked about two years old in the picture. Apparently, they used to correspond with each other frequently but that stopped as soon as Louisa married Herbert Flitch.

I asked her, "Did you ever meet Herbert?"

"No," she said, "but I knew his mother."

This came as a surprise to me, as I knew nothing about Mrs Flitch's background and I certainly did not know that she and my great aunt were acquainted.

"She was Lucretia Griffin before she married Horace Flitch. He was an accountant," she said. "Lucretia always had a shocking temper and he was a wrong 'un. He went to prison for fiddling the books at one of the shipyards where he worked. He must have served his time by now, but no one has seen hide nor hair of him since he went down and remember, Bettina, I'm in the business where we hear what's going on, particularly concerning deaths.

"Lucretia owns a house in Newcastle," she went on. "Gets a good rent, so I'm told, but she pleads poverty. Reckons she's a poor widow but, as far as I know, Horace Flitch is still alive, just not around. She's such a bitch who can blame him.

"Herbert Flitch was always in trouble as a lad but it's no wonder with a mother like that. Dreadful mother she was; used to lock him out and she even threw a bucket of cold water over him from an upstairs window as a punishment when he was just a little bairn. He hardly ever went to school and the police were never away from their door. The only thing he seemed to like, and he was good at, was playing the violin, but his mother smashed it one day as a chastisement for something or other.

"Mind you," Eliza Jane said, "He was quite a good looking boy and he fancied himself as a ladies' man, but I will tell you this Bettina with my hand on my heart, I thank God that neither of my girls took a shine to him."

I was really growing to love my aunt and it wasn't just her cooking, which was wonderful, but for her warmth, her humour and her love of a good chat.

CHAPTER 13

Letticia Ann

One afternoon whilst we were happily enjoying each other's company in the morning room I asked Aunt Eliza Jane if she would tell me about her sister, Letticia Ann. There had always been an air of mystery around my grandmother and I had never been able to persuade my mother or Vera to tell me much about her.

My aunt said that if I was absolutely sure, then she would be happy to. My response was positive, and I hope encouraging.

"As the older sister by some twelve years," she said, "I always felt responsible for Letticia Ann, who came to live with me following the death of our mother.

"She was an incredibly beautiful girl, if a little high spirited, with curly hair the colour of a golden sovereign and freckles on her nose, which she hated by the way. I did tend to spoil her, and if she wanted a new dress, I found it hard to say no.

"Now Bettina, I'm sure you are aware that not every woman looks good wearing black, it can be quite draining on the complexion. Your grandmother could wear any colour, but in black she looked stunning. She had a lovely calm way with her, and she started to work in our business in the front office reception as a funeral organiser, always wearing black. Jack, my husband, was very happy to have her on board as, at the time, my girls were quite young, so I was very busy at home.

"Letticia Ann took to the job like a 'duck to water' and the clients loved her as she just had a perfect way with them; empathetic I think you would call it.

"That's how she met your Grandfather, Tobias Pym who was thirty years her senior, when he came into the office to arrange the funeral for the first Mrs Pym. Letticia Ann was marvellous at organising funerals and he was delighted with the arrangements she made.

"Tobias wanted the very best for his wife, no expense spared, so we pulled out all the stops to give him a show. You know the kind of thing Bettina, the glass hearse with four black horses, each with a plume of black Prince of Wales feathers on its head. I had the impression that he wanted a bit of a theatrical production to impress all his business friends.

"So delighted was Tobias that he came back to the office about a month later to thank Letticia Ann and he invited her to go to the Theatre Royal to see the ballet; Swan Lake I think it was. Her answer was yes! This surprised me as he was so much older, by thirty years, which I'm sure you would agree is a big age gap. They did seem to enjoy each other's company and he was a very generous suitor with plenty of gifts for her and even occasionally a gift for me.

"A year after the first Mrs Pym had died, almost to the day, they were married in the cathedral and she became the second Mrs Pym, wearing a most beautiful white gown and handmade Carrickmacross needle-lace veil. The lady who gave the veil to me had no daughters and both her sons were killed in the first Boer war in South Africa. I still have the veil if ever you need it. It's the one Louisa wore when she married your father.

"Tobias Pym was a well-known businessman with a house in the country, out Hexham way, and a big terraced house here in Newcastle. As I told you Letticia Ann was always spoilt and here she had found a husband who enjoyed spoiling her and she loved it, at first. They often went to the theatre and she enjoyed being the hostess whenever he entertained guests, usually out at the Hexham house and for each function she usually had a new gown. She loved her clothes your Grandmother; always in the latest fashion. It didn't stop there, oh no! Tobias bought her French perfume and gorgeous jewellery, big diamonds and rubies mostly, I seem to remember."

"Did you ever stay with them in their country house," I asked.

"No, only a visit once and, if I'm honest, I found the place, Ford House it was called, rather dark and creepy. I did not want to sleep there and I did wonder if it was haunted but I said nothing about that to Letticia Ann. What I did detect however was that my sister was unhappy, and that the marriage was not a love match.

"Letticia Ann began to spend more and more time at the town house whilst Tobias stayed in the country, even before she had her girls. There was always a carriage, horse and groom at her disposal, so she would just turn up with her maid in tow. Tobias and Letticia Ann were married for eight years before Vera was born and Louisa came along two years later and still her residence of choice continued to be the town house, bringing in more staff to look after the children.

"One day we received word that Tobias Pym had dropped down dead out at his house in the country. Vera was seven years old and Louisa five years old and they were staying, with their mother, a governess and other staff in the town house. Your grandfather was sixty-five years old at the time of his death and we arranged his funeral, even though normally we would not go that far out of the city, but for family we made an exception.

"Jack, as head of the business, went over to Ford House to deal with things and all he would tell me was that it was a very funny set-up. When I asked him to elaborate, all he would say was that he thought that there was something strange and unnatural going on regarding the circumstances of Tobias's passing, adding 'don't ask me anything else because the less you know the better.'

"It turned out that Tobias had gone bankrupt and everything had to be sold. However, much to Letticia Ann's amazement and relief, before his death he had put a considerable amount of money into a bank account for her and the town house was now in her name. So, at least she and her girls had a roof over their heads.

"Managing a big town house was fine at first, but the money began to dwindle, and the staff had to be let go. Instead of a governess Vera and Louisa went to school which, personally, I thought was better for them because they made friends and became more outgoing.

"Letticia Ann realised after a few years that she needed an income, so decided to turn the house into a bed and breakfast establishment. Tasteful business cards were printed advertising the B&B and these were distributed to the medical school which was part of Durham University, the Fleming Children's Hospital and the Royal Victoria Infirmary, which was newly opened.

"That's how Louisa met Agatha who was born with a hip problem and was referred to an orthopaedic specialist in Newcastle. Agatha and her mother needed to stay overnight and sometimes for several weeks if an operation was involved. This went on for a good few years and Letticia Ann and Mrs Dawson became good friends. Your mam was invited to the harvest supper on the farm in the war and that's how she met your dad.

"The bed and breakfast business did very well for Letticia Ann and she had many interesting people who stayed with her, including doctors, professors and lecturers who were visiting the medical school, as well as famous actors who came to perform at The Theatre Royal. Louisa was now settled in Little Laxlet and when

Vera went to work for the bank here in Ransington I think that your grandmother became lonely. She was only in her fifties and Letticia Ann was still very good looking. She always dressed in the height of fashion.

"One guest at the B&B was a visiting surgeon, lecturing at the medical school and demonstrating some new surgical techniques at the hospital. He stayed with Letticia Ann several times and they struck up a relationship. I accidentally met him once when I called to see her unexpectedly, but 'secretive' should have been her middle name and she certainly was about him. It was obvious that the relationship had taken off big time! They always seemed to be going to the races which was enjoyable, she told me, unconvincingly.

"One day she announced that they were engaged to be married and Keith, her now fiancé, did not wish to live in Newcastle but said he would build a house for them overlooking the sea in Norfolk.

"Little did I know at the time that it was her money he would be building the house with and that she had sold her B&B as a going concern, transferring all the money over to him. When I did find out, Letticia Ann told me that there was no attachment for her to the Newcastle property or its contents, as everything in the house had been chosen by the first Mrs Pym and she would be renting a room there until Keith Walter sent for her. The house he was having built, would be furnished completely with new furniture which would be of her choice.

"To say my suspicions were aroused was the understatement of the year and I started to make a few enquiries about Mr Keith Walter up at the hospital where we, as a family, were, and still are well-known, calling on a regular basis, being in the line of business that we were in. The Head Porter, whom I'd known for years, told me that there was no surgeon, visiting or otherwise, by the name of Keith Walter but they did have a surgical instrument salesman who used to call at the hospital to demonstrate to the surgeons, the latest instruments. The man was called Walter Keith, but they had not seen him for a couple of months.

"I didn't know how I was going to tell Letticia Ann, but tell her I must, as she was worried that Keith, as she knew him, had had an accident. Of course, at first, she didn't believe me and said she would travel to Kings Lynn where she had the address of his spinster sister with whom he lived.

"I went with her and believe me Bettina, Kings Lynn from here is a most awkward place to travel to, but I had booked us into what turned out to be a good hotel, so I knew we would have a bed for the night.

"We found the house and his 'sister' was as shocked as we were, as it turned out she was his wife who had not seen him either. The police tracked Walter Keith down and he went to prison for his crime, but the money was all gone, blown on gambling and investments that had gone belly-up.

"Letticia Ann was now penniless and homeless, so I took her home with me, but things were never the same again. She still had her jewellery which was then sold, and I could never quite understand why. She wanted to give me the money for her keep which I accepted, but I saved it, just in case it was ever needed. When my sister died, I divided the money between Vera and Louisa and that is all there is to tell," Eliza Jane concluded.

"What did my grandmother die of?" I asked Aunt Eliza Jane.

"A broken heart and TB," was her reply.

"Thank you for telling me Letticia Ann's story Aunt, I now understand why Mam and Vera never want to talk about it," I said.

"The thing to learn from this Bettina, is that if you ever own anything that is worth something, keep it in your name."

"Sound advice," I replied, "much appreciated Great Aunt!"

CHAPTER 14

The Dance

Monday was always wash day at Iona House so, whilst John and Alfie were eating their breakfast, I would light the boiler in the wash house and sort the dirty clothes ready for Mrs Scribbins. This had become a regular routine for me, but on this particular Monday morning, when I returned from taking the boys to school, she still had not arrived, which was unusual, and somewhat concerning.

"I suppose I'd better make a start then," I said to Mrs Handyside.

"Tell you what," she said, "give me the items for hand washing and I'll do them in the scullery."

I was very happy to hand to her all the woollen matinee coats, hats, mitts, booties and little blankets, which she took along with the Lux soap flakes, lightening the load for me.

The white wash was boiling away when I heard someone whistling a cheerful tune and then there was a knock on the wash house door.

A young man, who introduced himself as Henry Penny said, "I've brought a message from Mrs

Scribbins. She says to say sorry, but she won't be coming today because Mabel and her bairn have diphtheria. Mrs Scribbins thinks that they might have to go to the fever hospital they are that poorly."

This was shocking news but not a total surprise as I had heard that there had been several cases of diphtheria around where Mrs Scribbins lived. Mrs Handyside described that part of town as the slums where families were living in very overcrowded and unsanitary conditions. I had never been there myself.

I thanked Henry Penny for the message. I then said, "If you will excuse me, I must get on with the washing, as there is a lot to do."

"I'll give you a hand if you like," He said.

This took me by surprise, but a helping hand would be very welcome, I thought.

Henry was fit and strong so good at lifting the hot, wet clothes from the boiler into the zinc tub, where he possed them vigorously in the suds. He took off his cap, which he had been wearing at a jaunty angle. His face became as red as his braces with the heat in the wash house and the clothes seemed to fly, with his help, through the rinsing and mangling process. Between us, we soon finished washing all the clothes.

It was a fine, late September morning and together, we pegged out the full wash onto the clothesline which made it sag. In no time Henry located the clothes prop, demonstrated the strength in his biceps by flexing them and then telling me how strong he was. He then elevated the line to allow the washing to dry, with the benefit of the breeze.

I offered him a cup of tea.

"As a rule, I only works for cash, Penny's me name and it's pennies by nature, shame me name's not pound," he said laughing. "But for a pretty girl like you I'll settle for a cup of tea."

We drank our tea in the yard at the back of the wash house and Henry showed me the cleats in the soles of his boots, demonstrating how to make them spark on the stone flags. Was I supposed to be impressed I wondered!

He told me that he was looking for work but, apart from the occasional labouring job, he had been unsuccessful.

I asked him, "Have you tried for a job at the foundry?" As I'd heard that there were puddler's jobs vacant.

"Oh, I tried that once but I've got a bronchial chest, so I didn't last long at that."

"Hello, hello," a man's voice called. Then there was a loud knocking on the kitchen door.

I went around the corner to see Norman, the coalman standing there. He wore a leather cape and apron which were black with coal-dust, as was the rest of his clothing, his hands and his face.

"I've brought ten bags today," he said. "That lad I've taken on is as idle as the day is long. I'm just sick to death of having to knock him up out of bed for a day's work, so today I'm managing on my own."

He was not his usual cheerful self. Obviously fed up with the idle lad.

"Miss Bettina please would you watch the horse whilst I bring the coal in?" he asked me.

Fleur, the coalman's horse, was big, calm and as gentle as a lamb, so I was very happy to keep her company whilst Norman carried the sacks of coal from the cart and emptied them into the coal house. She enjoyed the carrot I gave her, and I patted and stroked the neck of this beautiful animal. Mr Handyside was always pleased if Fleur deposited some horse manure in the lane as he vowed that it was the perfect food for his roses. The horse obliged.

The coal delivery only took about fifteen minutes but in that time Henry Penny had persuaded Norman that he would be of more use to him than the idle lad he currently employed. As I waved them out of the lane, Norman and Henry were sitting side by side on the cart, behind the horse. I couldn't help thinking that Henry Penny was not backward in coming forward, as he now had a job delivering coal.

I said to Mrs Handyside, "Well that worked out well for those two, didn't it?"

She did not look very happy and all she said to me was, "Henry Penny, more like Flash Harry if you ask me."

She sucked in her breath, turned on her heel and went off to vacuum the stairs.

Stan was faring well as a gardener and now had three gardens to look after, as well as helping his father with the gardening work at Iona House.

"Recommendation by word of mouth," his mother told me, often!

Stan's expertise was in pruning shrubs, trimming trees and he had even been known to fell trees, which was tricky, as obviously the tree had to fall away from any buildings. Our trees were well maintained, and he would saw the branches into logs and then stack them in the log store. Stan needed to carry his tools from job to job, so had made a wooden box cart which he had fixed to the back of his bicycle, which was ideal.

John and Alfie loved Stan to meet them at the end of their school day and give them a lift home, one sitting in the cart and the other on the crossbar of the bike, a 'croggie' they called it. When Stan met them there was always a stop at Granny Hughes sweet shop in Parliament Street for a sherbet dip or two ounces of humbugs. However, I had told Stan that the boys were not allowed gob stoppers, as I had a fear of one of them choking.

Rumour had it that the sweet shop was infested with mice but I had never seen any, perhaps that was because the shop's cat, Tolstoy, was known to be an excellent hunter and I'd heard him described by some as 'a mean looking bugger!'

I was just starching Uncle Angus's loose collars when Stan called to see me, which was a surprise, as I

135

wasn't expecting him but he was a welcome distraction from something I knew that I wasn't good at. Mrs Scribbins could starch and iron collars to perfection, but my efforts were somewhat lacking.

Stan said, "Bettina, I know how much you enjoy all the singing and dancing when we watch a musical, so how would you like to go to a proper dance?"

I thought this to be an exciting idea, but said, "I'd love to but I'll have to check with Auntie Vera first."

"You don't think I'll have to have another interview with Mr McLeod, do you?" Stan said, feigning a worried look.

"I hope not," I said.

We both laughed at the thought of it, but I know Stan did not find it funny at the time.

Vera wanted to know where the dance was, when the dance was, what time the dance was and I was able to answer all her questions, which meant I could go, so long as I was home by ten thirty p.m.

She then went on to say, "Angus and I love to dance."

This took me totally by surprise as I had no idea they were dancers.

"Oh yes." She went on, "Before we had a family, we used to go to the Metropole Hotel for cocktails and then to a dinner dance. Why don't you pick out some dance records Bettina and then tomorrow I can teach you some steps?"

The gramophone was in the morning room with a box of records which I looked through and found several which sounded like dance music, the big band sound and some jazz. Often the label indicated the appropriate dance for that record.

Vera was very keen to teach me to dance and said that she would take the man's role and lead; 123, 123 we counted as we waltzed round the room, which was not so difficult, I thought. She tried to teach me the Foxtrot, which she told me was hers and Angus's favourite dance, but to me it seemed rather advanced for a beginner. One record said 'Charleston' on the label which I had heard of but was unsure what kind of a dance it was.

"Put it on, I love it," Vera said.

I wound up the gramophone and placed the needle onto the spinning record and some very jazzy music began to play. Vera was in her element with the Charleston, giving it her all, and because she understood the rhythm of the music and knew the steps by heart, she moved really well.

The sound of the music had woken Claudette from her nap and when I brought her downstairs she was delighted to be held and danced round the room to the music.

'I Wanna Be Loved By You' was the song playing. Vera's hair had tumbled down from her plait with all the exertion, but she cradled her daughter in her arms whilst dancing. We both joined in with the song and Claudette squealed with delight.

Stan and I went by tram to the dance which was in a college hall in town. On the journey, Stan explained that he would like the first and the last dance with me but if I wanted to dance with any other boys in between, then that was fine with him. I suppose that was the etiquette of the dance hall, but he did not use that word. When we arrived at the college, we left our outdoor coats on the wooden seats which rose from a platform in a lecture theatre.

The vast, dimly lit dance room had a sparkly glitter ball in the centre of the ceiling and impressively, there was a live band, with a singer, on the stage. We found a table and Stan went to buy us both a lemonade, leaving me feeling isolated on my own as all the people around me seemed to know each other.

Stan soon returned, he bowed and said, "Madam, please may I have the pleasure of this dance?"

I was relieved that it was a waltz and I just kept counting 123, 123 as we twirled around.

I enjoyed watching others doing the Jitterbug and the Charleston, but I did not have the confidence to try them myself. Whilst watching, I observed another etiquette of the dance hall where it seemed that all the boys stood together at one end and the girls sat at the tables or they stood at the other end.

One dance, which was fun, had everyone in a circle doing the barn dance where we all changed partners as we went around; my poor feet were trodden on several times.

At one of the changes my new partner said, "Hello pretty girl, you're a long way from home." It was Henry Penny who did not stand on my feet. He was a very good dancer.

Later, the singer in the band announced that the next dance would be 'The Gay Gordons' which Henry asked me to partner him for.

"But I don't know it," I said.

He said, "Don't worry I do," whilst pulling me to my feet.

We whirled to the Scottish music and I just followed him, marching spinning and twirling, which I found great fun. He did not stand on my feet once and he told me that he was now in regular work with Norman the coalman.

Stan had partnered a few other girls during the evening but as we had promised I had the last dance with him which was a slow dance with the lights turned even lower. He held me close and I liked it, but I could not help looking at some of the other couples and I noticed that they were kissing as they danced. 'Impressive,' I thought, 'they must know the dance off by heart if they can kiss at the same time.'

We caught the tram back and Stan walked me to my door.

"Thank you," I said. "I've had a wonderful evening."

"Me too," he said.

He then kissed me on the cheek.

I looked into his kind face and into his eyes, and then I took the initiative and kissed him full on the mouth.

He must have enjoyed it because that first kiss lasted a long time.

CHAPTER 15

Evaleen

When Rory was about a month old, Great Aunt Eliza Jane returned home, to be with her daughters. I knew I would miss her and the times we spent together sewing. Percy drove her home in the Bentley and true to form, she gave us the Royal wave as the car pulled away.

My hexagons rarely came out of their box after that, as Vera needed more help with the cooking, and I was still in charge of the Monday wash and the Tuesday ironing. I had promised my great aunt that I would correspond with her, even though, at the time of the promise, I was unsure as to whether I would find the time.

Mrs Scribbins came back to work after three weeks and she told us that her granddaughter, aged eighteen months, had died from diphtheria, Mabel, her daughter, had survived but had lost the baby she had been expecting.

I thought that Mrs Scribbins was very stoical about the situation as she said, "Just one of those things I suppose. Mabel 'as been told by the 'ospital that 'er 'art might be weak now, so it's best she doesn't 'av any more bairns. So, I've told 'er — keep away from men."

Sometimes on a Saturday, I would meet Stan and we would take John and Alfie to the park where they liked to feed the ducks and play on the swings. On this Saturday there was to be a jumble sale in the Boy Scouts hut which was on the other side of the park to Iona House. I liked to be early for a jumble sale, so as to have first pick at the bargains and was always on the lookout for pretty patterned cotton dresses which I could cut up to cover the paper hexagons for my quilt. Occasionally I would find a dress or a jacket which fitted me so perfectly that I would wear it first, which was something I'd learned from Mam.

Stan called for us at about nine a.m. The boys were full of energy and ready for a game of football with him in the park. He had said that he would look after them while I went into the scrum of the jumble sale, where I really loved to rummage and I certainly did not hold back with my elbows, to find my way to the front of the tables.

As we walked through the park, I noticed one of the nannies, in full uniform, sitting on a bench.

'It's early for her to be here,' I thought, 'and she doesn't have any children with her.'

As we drew closer, I noticed that her coat buttons were all done up wrongly and that her hair was hanging very untidily beneath her hat, which was almost falling off. I found this very strange as the nannies, without exception, were always smart.

We were almost past her when I could see that she had been crying and was as white as a ghost, so I stopped, and sat beside her on the bench.

"Is something wrong?" I asked her. "Can I help you, are you feeling poorly?"

"I've walked out," she whispered. "I need to get home." Her voice was barely audible.

"Where do you live?" I asked.

"Huddersfield," was her reply, adding, "I have no money, I don't know what to do."

She was shaking and cold, so I asked Stan if he would play with John and Alfie in the park while I tried to find out what the problem was and hopefully could help this traumatised young woman. He was happy to do this, and he ran off with the boys, all of them chasing the football.

"My name is Bettina. What is your name?" I asked the Nanny.

"Evaleen Surtees," she replied.

"Have you had any breakfast," I asked.

"No," was her reply.

"Would you like to come home with me, and I will make you some?" I asked. She did not answer but just stared ahead looking frightened. I was unsure what to do next, but I remembered my mother holding my hand when I was scared, reaching out, I took her cold hand in mine.

Evaleen nervously looked around and then quietly she said, "I've been raped." There was no emotion in her voice at all. She then said, "Twice."

She looked frozen to the spot and for a while we sat in silence, with me holding her hand. Then I told her that the house where I lived was very close by and suggested she went back with me to the house where there would be privacy and I could give her some food and a warm drink.

Vera and Angus were going to his brother Ian's for the day so I knew that there would be no one else at home. Ian's wife, Dora, always insisted that visits to her home commenced early in the day, as this was her preference. She always had something new in her fabulous house to show visitors.

Never having been in such a situation before, I was very unsure as to what to do. My head was spinning with thoughts.

'Does Evaleen need to see a doctor? Is this a police matter? How will she get home?' I asked myself as I continued to hold her hand, walking slowly back to Iona House.

Once in the warm kitchen, I made tea and toast for us both, after offering her a poached egg; but she said that she wasn't hungry. We sat by the Aga and she told me that her employers were horrible unkind people. Then she went on to tell me about the family and what had happened to her.

"Mrs Perryman, mother of a baby and two other children, rarely went out of the house unless accompanied by her husband. There were many rules and regulations regarding when eating was allowed, which rooms Evaleen could go into, and when she could take a bath or do her laundry. Worst of all, she had not been paid any wages at all since she had started to work there, three months before.

Mr Perryman was a bank manager and frugal in the extreme with money; not allowing his wife any cash of her own or even to have an account with a shop; which meant that all the trades people who delivered to the house were paid by him, monthly. He kept a full and tight control of the household budget and there was rarely a fire in the grate or any hot water.

Mrs Perryman's clothes were made with fabric of his choice, by a dressmaker who came to the house. He supervised all the purchases of clothing bought for the children. There were never any visitors, but occasionally Mrs Perryman could be heard talking to her mother on the telephone. She always seemed nervous and the calls were short.

Worst of all, was that Mr Perryman never missed an opportunity to rub himself up against Evaleen and to grope her, sometimes even when his wife was in the room. He was cunning though and his wife did not see it. Once he ran his hand up Evaleen's leg under her clothes in front of his wife, who could not actually see what he was doing as they were all sitting at the table.

When Evaleen had looked across at Mr Perryman, during the incident, he had winked at her when his wife looked away to speak to one of the children.

"The children," she said, "were lovely and it felt sad to be leaving them. The oldest child had once told her that they had had a lot of nannies." Evaleen went on to say, "Last night, I was told by Mrs Perryman that there was some hot water and that I could have a bath. As usual, I was always very careful to lock the bathroom door before I started to run the bath and undress.

"I then thought I heard the big bathroom cupboard door creak. I noticed that it was slightly ajar, so I went to close it. As I did so, the cupboard door was pushed open from the inside and Mr Perryman stepped out into the bathroom wearing only his vest and in an obvious state of sexual excitement.

"'Do not even think of calling for help, shouting or screaming,' he said, in a sinister tone whilst moving towards me," Evaleen said.

"I started to scream, and he pushed me hard against the towel rail and I stumbled, hurting my back as I hit the edge of the bath. I lashed out with my fists, my knees and my feet, kicking and trying to fight him off. I know that I gouged his face and his nose before he managed to pin me down as he growled at me, 'Sodding bitch, clawing me like that. I'll make you pay for what you've just done. You are a whore and a temptress,' he kept repeating, as he raped me. His blood dripped from his face onto me, it even ran into my mouth. It was disgusting.

"Afterwards, he unlocked the bathroom door and left. I noticed that the bath wasn't even full, it had all happened so quickly. I was numb and too afraid to have a bath, so I just pulled out the plug and watched the water drain away, then went to my bedroom and I locked myself in.

"At about seven a.m. this morning Mrs Perryman was in the kitchen and I informed her that I was leaving, and asked for the wages which were due to me. 'What wages!' she shrieked. 'If you leave without serving your notice you are not entitled to any wages or money of any kind. Now just leave and do not come back or ever think of asking my husband for a reference.'

"It was very early, and I did not know where else to go," Evaleen said. "I walked from the house and saw that the door to the church was open, so I went in.

"The priest was giving Mass to a small congregation, so I sat near them. The service was soon over, and the people left but I didn't know what to do so I just sat there.

"The priest came over to me and asked if I wanted anything and could he help me.

"I told him that I had left my employer and asked if he could possibly lend me money for my train fare home and I would be sure to return it to him.

"He said, 'I am the priest here and if you just go into my sacristy over there, I will join you soon and we will see what I can do.'

"I went through the door he had pointed out to me, which led into a small office with a desk, there was a chair in front of the desk where I sat and waited.

"He came into the sacristy through a different door and sat in a chair behind his desk and said, 'I'm surprised that you have terminated your employment as jobs are hard to find these days due to the depression.'

"I had always been told that a priest will never betray a confidence," Evaleen said, "so I thought that it would be safe to tell him that Mr Perryman had assaulted and raped me in the bathroom last night and that Mrs Perryman had refused to give me the wages I was owed this morning.

"'I have always thought of Mr Perryman as a good man,' the priest said. 'A pillar of the community. How do I know that you are telling me the truth?'"

"But it is true," Evaleen told the priest, "It is absolutely true."

"I will need proof," the priest said.

"What do you mean proof?" Evaleen asked him.

"The priest answered in an authoritative tone, 'I will need to see the bruises for myself to confirm that you are not lying to me. Then and only then will I have the jurisdiction to lend you your train fare. I will go out of the room whilst you undress.'

"This had me worried," Evaleen said. "But I thought to myself, he is a man of God, so I should be able to trust him as though he was a doctor.

"When the priest returned, I had taken the top of my dress down to show him the bruises on my back where I had been pushed onto the towel rail then fell onto the edge of the bath."

"He said, 'Oh yes there is some definite bruising on your back,' running his fingers across the bruise at the same time.

"The next thing I knew he had a tight band around my neck and my face felt as though it would burst, I couldn't breathe and I must have fainted."

"As I regained consciousness, he was raping me, I could smell incense and all I could see was the crucifix on the sacristy wall. Then it was over.

"'You know you have been very wicked making me do this,' he calmly said, 'very wicked and very sinful. As for your lies about Mr Perryman, I do not believe you. In fact, I doubt anyone would, you could be committed to the lunatic asylum for besmirching the character of an honourable man.'

"As he was saying this, he slid his cincture from where it had been tied around my neck, he gently coiled it then lovingly placed it in a small case with his stole.

"I realised that he could have strangled me and although I felt terrified, I knew I had to get out of that church," Evaleen said.

"'Dress yourself and leave immediately, as I myself am leaving to give Mass to the housebound. If you are still here when I return, you will leave me no other option than to inform the police,' the priest said

"The last I saw of him was his back as he went out of the sacristy door and into the aisle of the church where an almost imperceptible flurry of wind caused his long black cape to billow out like an evil sail of depravity," Evaleen said, without any emotion.

She then told me that she dressed very quickly, left the church and sat on the park bench which was where I had found her.

It was difficult to take in all that she had just told me, and I wished that Vera or aunt Eliza Jane were there, as they would know what to do.

Evaleen kept stressing over and over that she did not want anyone to know about the rapes, as she felt such a strong sense of shame. All she wanted to do was to go home to her mother.

I asked her, "Would you like to have a bath here? I know there is hot water."

She said that she would, and I ran her a bath, putting the last few of my Yardley's lavender bath salts into the water. At her request, I stayed with her and locked the bathroom door because she was shaking and in shock.

When she was in the bath, I could see the huge linear bruises across her back, and the bruising on her shoulder and on her arms and wrists. All around her neck, there was a deep red mark, with bruising beginning to appear around it. I noticed that there was some petechiae bruising to her cheeks; I concluded that she was lucky to be alive.

"Would you like to see a doctor," I asked.

Her response was immediate, "No, no, no, I don't want to end up in the asylum."

She picked up a nail brush and scrubbed at her fingers until they were red and we both noticed bits of skin which had been trapped under her long, strong well-manicured fingernails fall into the bath water.

When Evaleen was dry, I lent her a clean nightdress and she climbed into my bed. I told her she was safe now and that I would try to figure out a way to get her back to Huddersfield.

I could hear that Stan and the boys were home, so I told her to lock the bedroom door if she wanted to, as I now needed to go to see to John and Alfie.

The boys were growing fast and they had very healthy appetites. They said they were starving and all four of us tucked into bacon, eggs and fried bread.

After lunch, John and Alfie went into the morning room to play with the train set and I was able to explain to Stan all that Evaleen had told me, stressing the importance of confidentiality.

We decided that for her to travel by rail alone would not be appropriate, as she would be very nervous about being in a carriage with a male passenger. Also, the next day there would only be a Sunday train service, which would complicate matters even more.

Stan said, "I think I'll ask Percy if I can borrow his car and then we could both take her back to Huddersfield tomorrow."

I thought that was a good idea, but Stan was still only learning to drive, and Percy was, understandably, protective about his own little car.

Vera, Angus and the babies returned from their outing to Ian and Dora's.

"That woman exasperates me," Vera said, meaning Dora and looking pleased to be home. "Her house is immaculate and she didn't move any of her precious Ming vases, not even one. It was a nightmare, Claudette wanted to touch everything, and I could see that Dora was on edge."

Vera then impersonated Dora, "Your children will need to learn self-control, I don't believe in moving anything." She sounded just like Dora.

"Moving anything, moving anything, I'm a nervous wreck," Vera said.

Angus disappeared into his study and I did not quite know how I was going to break the news to Vera that Evaleen was upstairs in my bed.

I need not have worried as Alfie came into the room and said, "There's a nanny upstairs."

Evaleen had been crossing the landing to go to the toilet and Alfie had recognised her.

I explained to Vera that Evaleen had left her employment, which was not far from Iona House, due to the many problems but I did not mention the rapes, rather more of an outline of the situation.

"You did the right thing Bettina. You couldn't just leave the girl sitting in the park, now could you?" she said.

Vera then went on to say that if Percy agreed to lend Stan his car then she and Angus would look after the boys while we took Evaleen home.

"An afternoon at the coast will be just the thing." She went on, "The sea air will help me to forget the awful day we've just had at Dora's."

'John and Alfie will enjoy a trip to the beach too,' I thought.

Stan called round later that evening and he gave me the news that, although Percy was at first reluctant about lending his car, when Stan explained to him about Evaleen's situation, without breaching confidentiality, he readily agreed. We both thought that we would need to make an early start the following morning, so we had a brief kiss and said goodnight.

I made myself a shaky down bed on the floor next to my bed with spare bedding from the linen cupboard, a pillow and an eiderdown. I then gave Evaleen the good news about taking her home tomorrow whilst we drank our hot cocoa. She looked relieved and I hope she slept. I know I did.

CHAPTER 16

Huddersfield

Percy couldn't lend Stan his car as he realised that he had promised to take his sister to visit a friend in hospital. However, he did know a good mechanic who had a van for sale. He'd had a word with him and arranged for Stan to hire the van for the day.

Evaleen and I were ready to travel to Huddersfield by eight a.m. when Stan knocked on the kitchen door and said, "Your carriage awaits ladies."

I could not believe my eyes when I saw the vehicle in the back lane, it was an ex Huntley and Palmer's delivery van. The writing on the side of the van had been roughly painted out and to me it looked like a bit of an old boneshaker with only two seats. I must have looked disappointed.

"Not to worry," Stan said. "Sound as a bell, all aboard girls."

In view of the awful day Evaleen had experienced the day before, I suggested she should sit in the front, alongside Stan. I climbed into the back and tried to make myself comfortable on an old armchair, which was bolted to the van floor.

I had packed sandwiches in greaseproof paper and a flask of tea, as we were not sure how long the journey would take. Percy had insisted on lending Stan two petrol cans which he had filled with petrol and had also given him a map. Evaleen asked if she could navigate as this would take her mind off things. Stan started the van and we were on our way.

Although he had only had a few driving lessons with Percy, Stan seemed to be very confident and luckily there wasn't much traffic on the roads, as it was a Sunday morning.

About an hour into the journey Evaleen complained that she was feeling nauseous, so we played 'I Spy' to take her mind off it. This worked for a while, but eventually we had to stop as she looked ashen with a tinge of green and I did not want her to vomit in the hired van.

We parked on the grass verge. Stan topped up the petrol tank while I set out a little picnic for us on a rug where we sat and enjoyed a cup of tea. I think that our driver was ready for a break.

Evaleen said, "I'm very grateful to you both, I couldn't bear to stay in Ransington a moment longer, I just want my mam."

Back in the van, we kept heading south with Evaleen reading the map and navigating for us, which gave her a focus as she was on her way home. I had the definite impression that she needed to put as many miles as possible between herself and Ransington. Arriving in

Huddersfield, Evaleen directed us to her home which was a ground floor flat in a terraced street.

Stan parked the van and immediately, about ten children gathered round. They wore dirty, tattered clothes, some with no shoes, a couple of them had rickets and they all had dirty, matted hair.

"I'll guard your van for a tanner mister," the biggest boy said to Stan.

Before Stan could answer, the door of Evaleen's flat opened and an incredibly good-looking young man, aged about twenty came out onto the pavement.

"This is my brother John," Evaleen said.

"If there's as much as a scratch on that van I'll scalp the lot of you," he said to the children. He added, "Keep your eye on it though and I'll give you some bottles to take back later."

Evaleen ran straight into the flat and into the arms of her mother. They were not expecting her home, so she quickly explained that she had left her employment, but she did not go into all the details. From the expression on her mother's face I could tell that she was concerned as she knew that her daughter would not have suddenly left her job as a nanny without a good reason. There was a wonderful smell of roast beef in the flat and we were invited to stay for Sunday dinner.

John and Stan were quickly into deep conversation about cars, rugby and football and the ragged children continued to guard the van. I asked if I might visit the toilet before we sat down to eat and Evaleen took me down some steep stone steps into the back yard, where there was a brick shed inside which was a flush toilet, which, she explained, they shared with the people who lived in the flat above them. The arrangement with the neighbour upstairs was that Mrs Surtees kept the toilet fresh and clean and that the man upstairs provided vegetables from his allotment in return.

We all sat down at the table where we were served a huge Yorkshire pudding each, all by itself on a plate. The enormous jug of gravy, which looked and smelt delicious, was offered to me first, I supposed it was because I was a guest. I wondered if this was the meal itself, but it was only the starter, as tender roast beef followed with at least five different vegetables, followed by a portion of perfectly 'baked in the oven' rice pudding, which had a crisp golden skin on the top.

Evaleen was quiet during the meal but I was pleased to see that she did eat some of her mother's beautifully cooked food. Conversation flowed between the rest of us and Mrs Surtees told us that she was a widow and that her husband had been killed in action in the Great War. Stan commented that he was amazed that she was still single as she made prize winning Yorkshire puddings and gravy.

She said, "I'm very flattered Stan, but I have a small war pension which I would lose if I remarried. In fact, I'm better off than most of the families in this street."

"Evaleen had once considered becoming a librarian," Mrs Surtees told us, "but her fondness for children had led her to make a career decision to become a nanny."

She had told me of her love of books, and I wondered if she might now reconsider and look for employment at the library.

Mrs Surtees then went on to tell us that she herself had a part-time job at the corner shop, which suited her well. John told us that he played rugby league for a local amateur team, which did not surprise me as he was very muscular. His mother also told us that he was a champion arm wrestler, down at the working men's club, however Stan declined the offer of an arm-wrestling contest with him and we enjoyed the good-humoured banter around the table.

I was taken with John's handsome good looks. I forced myself not to stare at him, which was what I wanted to do. His mother joked about girls beating a path to the door which he just brushed off, although I did think he looked rather embarrassed.

I had the definite impression that this was a very close good-humoured family and Evaleen would now receive all the support that she needed and I wondered if she would ever tell her mother and brother, the details of why she had returned home so suddenly.

John told us that he worked for a company in Huddersfield that made electric motors, as did his cousins. Thankfully, they all thought their jobs were as secure as any, in this time of depression.

John enquired about the amount of petrol we were carrying and a joint decision was made between him and Stan that the spare petrol cans should be refilled as we might need to refuel on the journey home and Sunday was the day when some petrol stations closed early. They went off together to meet John's friend who had a garage and the cans were topped up. To me the two men appeared to have struck up a good friendly rapport, probably based on cars and sport.

We thanked Mrs Surtees for her hospitality and John for the petrol. Evaleen gave me a big hug and then we drove out of Huddersfield, heading north for home.

It was so much nicer sitting in the front of the van next to Stan, rather than on the rickety old armchair in the back. Whilst we drove along, Stan told me of his plans, which made me realise that he was quite ambitious, a fact I had been unaware of until then.

"Bettina," he said. "One day I will be running my own business."

"What kind of business?" I asked.

"Well," he said. "At the moment, as you know, I do the gardens for three houses and I know the country is still in a depression but there is money about. It's just a question of tapping into it."

"Does this mean you are planning to expand your gardening business?" I asked.

"There is money about Bettina. Just look at Ian and Dora in that great big house of theirs. There must be loads more like them, loads more!" Stan said.

"Yes," I said. "But tell me exactly, what is this plan of yours?"

He answered, "If I had a van then I would paint on the sides Stanley Handyside, Tree Specialist and Gardener and then put a telephone number.

"I reckon that's where the money is; in tree work, lots of people have big trees growing near their houses, with branches which are often in need of a trim."

I had not realised he was so ambitious and although I felt full of admiration, I did wonder how he was going to afford to buy a van.

It was lovely, just driving along, chatting together without the responsibility of having the boys in tow.

"Do you have any ambitions?" Stan asked me.

"I haven't really thought about it," I said. "I know that I will need to have a job and earn an income, but it has been so busy at Iona House that there hasn't even been time for me to look."

"I can see you as a teacher," Stan said.

"A teacher, I don't know about that," I said. "But one thing I do know is that I'd prefer that to being a washerwoman. It's too much hard work."

We laughed and chatted together as the miles went by. I found it so relaxing to be with Stan, just the two of us on the open road.

"Did you see that sign?" I asked him.

"I did," he said. "Would you like to stop?" The sign had said,

FRESH EGGS FOR SALE.
PEACOCK FEATHERS FOR SALE.

Stan followed the arrows leading us down a long farm track, opening into a farmyard which fronted an old stone farmhouse. Chickens scattered as we drove in but other than that there did not seem to be anyone about.

A cat, sitting on a windowsill was seriously grooming itself. It took a moment to acknowledge our arrival. As we stepped out of the van, a collie dog came running towards us, barking, I hoped it was friendly. The collie was followed by a lurcher, followed by a Jack Russell, which made more noise than the other two dogs combined. A woman came out of the farmhouse. She looked a work weary forty in her wellingtons, with cord trousers tied up with bailing twine, and an old tweed jacket and cap. The cat returned to the grooming of its rear end.

It was the distinctive smell of the country which hit my senses as we walked towards her, bringing back memories of my childhood. Having lived in the country all my life until a year ago when I moved to Ransington, this wonderful aroma took me right back to my happy days with Louisa in Groat Cottage and suddenly I felt homesick for Little Laxlet before the Flitches came into our lives.

"Is it eggs thas come for?" the woman asked, which brought me back to reality.

"Yes," Stan replied, "and we would also be interested in buying a cup of tea, if you sell teas."

"How many eggs does't tha want?" she brusquely asked.

"Two dozen if you have them," Stan said.

He would take a dozen for his mother and a dozen for me to take for Vera.

"Follow me then," the woman said.

We did and she took us into a clean cool room which she told us was the dairy. The eggs were packed for us and Stan paid her.

There was no mention of tea, but then she said, "If thas thirsty there's watter in't pump ower there, help yoursen."

The woman then, without even saying goodbye, walked back into the stone farmhouse. She was terse, even by Yorkshire standards. Stan and I looked at each other and had a fit of the giggles.

"Which charm school do you think she went to?" he jokingly said, and we giggled some more.

We were just about to get back into the van with our eggs when a girl on a pony came into the farmyard.

"Hello," she said. "Is anyone looking after you?"

She dismounted and told me that it was fine to pat the pony whose name was Jesse.

"I'm Dolly," the girl said, smiling. "Have you come to buy peacock feathers?"

"We came for eggs," Stan and I said together.

"Would you like to see the peacock?" she asked.

We thought that it might look churlish if we said no so we agreed.

"I'll just put Jesse inside his stable then, if you can hang on, we can go and find George," Dolly said.

She took us into a field behind the farmhouse where first we saw a peahen with colouring so modest it blended in with the hedgerow. Her mate, George, was magnificent, the blues and greens of his feathers were iridescent and his long tail feathers trailed for some length behind him.

We complimented Dolly on her splendid peacock and his peahen and she then told us that she had called him George after the king, but the peahen was just Peahen.

As if on cue, George fanned his tail feathers, shaking them impressively giving a spectacular display in an attempt to interest his mate who seemed totally uninterested.

"I don't think I've ever seen anything so beautiful," I said to Stan. "I've only seen pictures of a peacock in a book before."

"Me neither," he said, as he took hold of my hand. It was quite a unique and special moment for us both.

"I sell the feathers for charity," Dolly said.

"In that case we will just have to buy some," Stan said.

The girl explained that the money she raised from selling the feathers she gave to the local cottage hospital that was raising funds for a children's ward. She then went on to tell us that her little brother, who was only ten years old, had a TB spine and that he was in hospital way out on the moors.

"It seems so wrong for him to be all alone so far away. My mam and my dad only get to see him once a month. If we had a children's ward at the cottage hospital, he could be nearer and not be so lonely," she said.

I asked Dolly her age and she said that she was thirteen years old.

"I'm very sorry to hear about your little brother being ill and so far away from home," I said. "That must make your parents sad."

"It does," Dolly said with great expression, "And what makes it worse is that my dad has an ingrowing toenail that makes him almost impossible to live with, he'll be steeping his feet in the big puddy dish now before he has to get on with the afternoon milking."

Out of interest, I naively asked Dolly what a puddy dish was.

She answered, "It's the huge dish we make the Christmas puddings in."

We were about to depart when Dolly said, "I make and sell lemon curd as well, all for the children's ward."

164

So, of course we bought two jars of lemon curd, as well as some peacock feathers.

Dolly acted as a most competent guide for Stan as he performed a three-point turn in the farmyard. We waved goodbye, once again heading for home.

Stan said, "I'm relieved she wasn't selling Christmas puddings."

I said, "I couldn't agree more, how yucky is that, puddings and an ingrowing toenail in the same dish."

For some reason this made us laugh and the rest of the journey was relaxing and enjoyable. Stan was such a good driver, that I felt at ease beside him and I knew that we were both pleased to have taken Evaleen home to her family.

"Do you think she will ever tell them the full story?" I asked Stan.

"Who knows," he replied. "Maybe she will. Maybe she won't. We may never know."

Darkness was falling and we were almost back at Iona House when my thoughts turned to cleaning John and Alfie's boots and getting their clothes ready for school the following morning. I also knew I'd need to sort the washing and put some clothes in to soak, ready for Mrs Scribbins the next day.

"I'll just drop you at the door if that's okay, as I need to take the van back," Stan said.

"That's fine," I said. "I have a few things to do tonight myself."

I was also keen to hear how the day at the seaside had been for Vera, Angus and the children.

We had a brief peck of a kiss and then I went into the house with my eggs, peacock feathers and lemon curd.

CHAPTER 17

Hampton House

The day out at the beach had been a huge success, despite the biting October northeast wind. Vera and Angus had made the decision not to take the children onto the pier, but instead the sight of the almost deserted golden beach drew them, allowing the boys to run with total freedom. John and Alfie loved the sand and the rock-pools' contents held a real fascination for them, on their first visit to the seaside.

Vera said, "When Claudette saw John and Alfie taking off their shoes and socks, of course, she insisted on doing the same. All three of them paddled in the sea, squealing and jumping when a wave came near. Angus supported Claudette to stop her from falling in the water and lifted her over the waves. She loved it. As for Rory, well he was well wrapped up, snuggled under my cape and I fed him in the car."

"The walk on the beach was very bracing," Angus said. "I think we all have colour in our cheeks. We decided that a treat of afternoon tea was in order, so we all went to the Grand Hotel, and before you ask, Bettina, the boys were very well behaved."

I asked John and Alfie what they had enjoyed the most about their day at the seaside which caused them to put their heads together and have a whispered conversation.

Then John said, "Looking through the telescope which was in the window of the hotel. It was fantastic, the ships looked really close. We could even read their names."

Alfie nodded in agreement.

Angus predicted that the boys would sleep well after all that fresh sea air and he was correct. Their heads hardly touched their pillows before they were both sound asleep.

Later that evening, Vera recounted to me the time they had spent as Ian and Dora's guests the day before.

"I feel stressed just telling you about it," she said.

Angus poured Vera a sherry and he gently massaged her shoulders.

"As you know Bettina, Dora has her huge Chinese vases and many other delicate 'objets d'art', as she calls them," Vera said. "She refused to move anything or even to allow us to sit in the kitchen, even though I asked. Of course, with Claudette crawling, taking a few steps now and pulling herself up to stand on furniture, it was a nightmare. Rory was fine in his carrycot on wheels, but dear Dora insisted that Claudette be allowed to roam.

"Dora said, 'Let her explore and if she goes to touch anything then give her hand a good smack.'

"But you don't believe in smacking," I said.

"Oh, I know," Vera said. "I feel tense just thinking about it."

"Dora insisted that that was the way she had trained her boys and it had not done them any harm."

Vera went on to say that she had found the whole visit difficult so, after luncheon, as Dora called it, she suggested to Dora that a walk with Angus and the children would be just the thing, on the pretext that the new house building in the area was of interest to them.

"Dora's response was, 'That's a brilliant idea, you will be amazed at some of the huge and interesting houses we now have here at Mallard Hall. Nothing on less than a third of an acre. This area is beginning to be known as incredibly exclusive; only for those from the top drawer.'

"The walk was interesting," Vera said. "We could not believe how many new houses had been built since our last visit and Claudette really enjoyed sitting on her daddy's shoulders as we walked along, singing marching songs. We attracted a few funny looks but we didn't care, as it made such a welcome break from Dora's constant dialogue regarding her latest acquisitions."

Vera then said, "You'll never believe what Dora's latest purchase is."

"I cannot even begin to imagine," I said, rolling my eyes.

"A refrigerator," Vera said. "Only a flipping refrigerator," she repeated.

"When did she get that?" I asked.

"About two weeks ago and now she just cannot imagine life without it," Vera said. "Apparently it doesn't make ice, as the ones in America do, but just as soon as an ice making refrigerator is available in England Dora plans to have one. And she will."

"Such an asset for cocktail parties," Vera added, impersonating Dora.

I had only been to Dora and Ian's home, Hampton House, once, which was back in the summer before Rory was born. Claudette was not walking at the time, but I was worried about the boys who were both very lively and with all the precious objects in that house I was not even remotely confident that there would not be a breakage.

On that one and only visit, Dora said to me, "I have recently acquired this wonderful Christopher Dresser jardinière," as she pointed to a big green and yellow pot which was balanced on its tall green and yellow pedestal. "It is a very rare item and extremely valuable. We are so very lucky to have it, don't you agree Bettina, it goes so well with the parquet floors and panelled walls. Very 'Art Nouveau'." She went on, and on.

This made me feel even more nervous and uncomfortable, so I asked her if I could take John and Alfie into the garden to kick the ball about.

'They would then be away from the extremely valuable pot,' I thought.

"You may go into the garden," Dora said. "But do not kick the ball anywhere near my bedding plants or endanger my coloured leaded light windowpanes. I do not wish to see any damage."

This remark made me feel even more tense as I had a horrendous mental image of the ball smashing her landing window, which was of a yacht sailing into the sunset, very expensive no doubt, with its coloured leaded glass. I suggested a game of hide and seek to the boys as a way of passing time, which they accepted.

We had been instructed by Dora as to where in her three-acre garden we could play. However, five-year-old Alfie, who had not quite understood her rules, had wandered off into a different part of the huge garden and I could not find him, so I assumed, rightly as it happened, that he must be hiding elsewhere. The compost heap was where I eventually found him.

Dora looked very tight lipped and was inhaling deeply on her cigarette when we returned back indoors and although I'd brushed Alfie down with my hands, he still looked dishevelled and did not smell too good. Dora made no comment at the time.

Later that evening, when we had returned to Iona House, the telephone rang, and it was her wanting to speak to me.

In an angry tone of voice, she said, "And what do you think you were doing this afternoon?"

Not having a clue what she was talking about I said, "What do you mean, what was I doing? I was playing hide and seek with John and Alfie."

This was the only answer I could offer.

"Well I'll tell you what you were doing young lady!" she said. "You were trespassing! Yes, trespassing on my private terrace, and don't say you weren't because I saw you from the house!" Her voice was angry and rising as she spoke.

"My terrace is private!" she shouted down the phone. "It is for my personal use and for my family only, so what makes you think you have the right to go there is beyond me!"

She then went on to tell me that I was very lucky that Angus had agreed to allow Vera to take me, and 'those brothers of yours', as she referred to them, in and that I should be more grateful.

I was stunned. I seem to recall that my legs felt weak and shaky; for a moment I said nothing.

"Well!" she said. "Do you have anything to say for yourself?"

"I do," I said, trying to sound more composed than I felt following such a vitriolic verbal attack and knowing that I must choose my words carefully.

My reply to her was, "I can hear that you are upset Dora and for that reason I am sorry. However, I was unaware that any part of your garden was considered private. I am, of course, immensely grateful to Vera and to Angus for giving me and my brothers a home and I'm sure that my own mother would have done the same had our positions been reversed."

Silence at the other end of the telephone.

So, I continued, "Your house and your garden are incredibly beautiful Dora, perhaps a little fence around your personal terrace might be an idea, then you won't run the risk of non-family members walking across it." As this is all I had done whilst searching for Alfie.

As far as I was concerned that was the end of the conversation, so what she said next astounded me.

"You are right Bettina," Dora said in a calmer voice. "A pretty little picket fence would do the trick, I might have it painted white."

My attempt at sarcasm had completely gone over her head; just as well, as I had no wish to offend her further.

John, Alfie and I have never been invited back to Hampton House since.

From the way Vera had told me of her day there with Rory and Claudette things hadn't changed. What was a mystery to us both was that Ian was so devoted to Dora and that he refused her nothing.

I said, "Dora seems very spoilt to me. Has Ian always given her everything she wants?"

"Yes always," Vera said. "From the moment they met."

"Do you think he realises that she controls him and the children?" I asked.

"Well you know what they say," was her reply, "love is blind."

"Anyway, how did your trip to Huddersfield go?" Vera asked.

I told her about the trip and how kind and appreciative Evaleen's mother had been and that her brother, John was big, handsome and strong without, I hoped, giving away the fact that I found him attractive.

Vera seemed impressed that Stan had driven all the way there and back in an old Huntley and Palmer's van, so I then went on to tell her of his ambition to have his own business and to print his name on the side of his own van, if only he could raise the money to buy it.

"He could be right, you know," she said. "There are hundreds of new houses near where Ian and Dora live at Mallard Hall, all with huge gardens; just crying out for someone to plant them up and maintain them. Several of the houses backed onto woods and there was one property which seemed to have been built in an old orchard."

"Do you think it would be worth it for Stan to advertise in that area?" I asked.

"It is certainly worth a try," Vera said.

When I saw Stan the next day, I told him about the big new houses at Mallard Hall and we both thought that it would be a good idea to let it be known that he was a good gardener, but how?

There were no shops yet in that area; only a small café which, I understood, was popular.

"Shall I make a poster and ask the café if they would display it?" I said.

"Would you Bettina, that would be great," he answered. "Meanwhile I'll go to the Gazette office and enquire what the cost of an advertisement would be. Then I have that appointment at the bank tomorrow as that is the only way that I can buy a van, if I can raise a bank loan."

Although I had a great fear of debt, I had to agree with him that a bank loan would be the only solution, unless I could think of another one.

Disappointingly the bank turned Stan down for the loan because he wasn't established in his business and he did not have a bank account.

"Back to square one," he said' "If only we knew someone who was really, really rich."

"Well the only person I can think of is Ian," I said.

"Ian is a great man, but I'm not sure about asking him for a loan and what about Dora? Do you honestly think, for even one moment that she would agree?"

"Shall I see what Vera thinks?" I asked.

"No," Stan said. "If I'm going to ask Ian for a loan I don't want to involve others. I'll need to pluck up the courage and I haven't made up my mind yet."

What Stan had not said was that I could not contact Ian directly, so the next day I did. Not wanting Dora to answer the telephone I phoned Ian at his chambers, where a secretary answered, and told me that luckily Ian was available to talk to me.

"Hello Bettina, this is a surprise. I hope that everything is Okay," Ian said.

"Oh yes thank you everything is fine. I'm ringing on behalf of my friend Stan," I said.

Being a barrister Ian immediately assumed that Stan was in trouble and that he needed his advice. I assured him that this was not the case.

"Then why does your young man want to see me?" Ian asked.

Realising that he was a busy man, I outlined Stan's business plans, his need for a van and the reason why the bank had turned him down.

"Tell you what Bettina," Ian said, "I'm in Court for the rest of today but if Stan comes over here to my office, say at about nine thirty a.m. tomorrow, I can discuss it with him then."

I thanked Ian. I then realised that I needed to get a message to Stan to tell him about the appointment but I was not sure where he was working. Mrs Handyside knew so I borrowed an old bicycle from the garage and with directions from Percy, I cycled off to find Stan with the news. All the time hoping that my skirt would not become caught in the chain, or in the back wheel.

Stan, wearing his best cap and jacket, and feeling very nervous, met with Ian at the appointed time, in Ian's chambers which were near the Law Courts.

When Stan explained his business plans and the need for a van Ian said no to a loan of fifty pounds but then he went on to say.

"I like your business idea Stan, but you will need more than fifty pounds, there will be all kinds of costs that you have not even thought of."

Stan said, "I know Mr McLeod, but I thought that if I could only buy the van then I could earn more, pay you back and expand the business."

"Now this is what I propose," Ian said. "Listen to what I have to say then tell me what you think of my proposal."

Ian's proposal was to lend Stan one hundred and fifty pounds which would buy the van plus some essential equipment, such as a safety harness and a chain saw for the tree work. In return Ian would own thirty percent of the business which could be reviewed after one year.

He then went on to say that he would not require any repayments until the business was in profit. Proper accounts would have to be kept and there was a need for a bank account to be opened in the name of the business.

"I will be what is known as a 'silent partner' and we do not need to broadcast the fact," Ian said.

Stan interpreted this last comment as a sign that Ian's business proposal was not intended to be known about by anyone, including Dora.

Ian then gave Stan a cheque for one hundred and fifty pounds and advised him to open a bank account without delay. He also told Stan that he had a friend who was a company lawyer. He would draw up the necessary paperwork for them both to sign.

Stan realised that Ian had provided him with the opportunity of a lifetime; when most of the country was still enduring the effects of the depression.

CHAPTER 18

An Early Birthday Present

The following day I received two letters in the post. The handwriting on one envelope I recognised as being that of Great Aunt Eliza Jane, the other that of my friend Ada.

> *High Stones*
> *Gosforth*
> *Newcastle*
> *upon Tyne.*

> *October 20th,*
> *1932.*

My Dear Bettina,

Thank you for your letter. I arrived home safely following a most comfortable journey in the Bentley, chauffeured by Percy.

It was a joy for me to be staying at Iona House when baby Rory was born, and I sincerely hope that he is thriving. Have Claudette and the boys accepted the new baby?

Enclosed you will find a cheque for twenty pounds, which is made out to you. This is by way of being a birthday present, even though I know your seventeenth birthday is not for another month.

You may recall mentioning to me that you hoped that your mother's treadle sewing machine was still in the cottage at Little Laxlet and I know how much you wish you could have brought it with you, well your worries are now over my dear Bettina as, with this money you can now purchase a sewing machine of your very own, if you wish.

It may be of interest to you to know that Herbert Flitch is living here in Newcastle in his mother Lucretia's house, with his father Horace. There are also still tenants and lodgers in the property and I'm not sure what they are up to but, knowing Horace Flitch, it will be of ill found nature. My spies are everywhere and I will keep you informed of any developments.

Our family business has opened a new branch and we continue to prosper. We will be coming up to the busy season shortly.

Please convey my love and good wishes to Vera, Angus and the family.

As always,
Your loving Aunt,
Eliza Jane.

A cheque for twenty pounds, made out to Bettina Dawson, was in the envelope with the letter. I could not believe it. I was not sure how a cheque became money as I had only had cash before, but I did know that I would need a bank account.

Angus was working at home in his study that morning, so I was able to ask his advice.

"What a lovely surprise for you," he said. "An early birthday present. Do you have any plans for it?"

"I have," I said, "I'm hoping to buy a sewing machine."

"Well I don't know anything about sewing machines," Angus said, "but I do have an hour or so, to spare, if you want to, I can take you into the bank and you can open an account and deposit your cheque. It might be an idea to bring your birth certificate with you if you have it, but don't worry if you haven't, as I know all the bank staff well."

We were served by a charming lady bank teller who helped me to fill in the necessary forms. Uncle Angus sat on one of the leather sofas, having told me that he would leave me to it, unless I wanted him for anything.

Opening my bank account did not take long and I gave the teller my cheque. The amount was recorded in my bank book which I was given to keep. When I turned from the counter, I noticed that Angus was in conversation with a man wearing an eye patch. I walked over to join them.

"This is my niece Bettina," Angus said as he introduced me. "She has just opened an account here."

"Very pleased to meet you," the man said, shaking my hand. "I am Ernest Perryman, the Manager here. If there is ever anything you require help with, please do not hesitate to contact me personally. Your Uncle and I have been business acquaintances for many years."

"That is very kind of you, old chap," Angus said, "but you look as though you've been in the wars. Hope you gave the other fellow as good as you got, as they say."

"Oh this," Perryman said, pointing to his eye and face which looked as though the deep, now healing, injury might leave him scarred. "It's nothing much, a tree branch hit me in the face that's all. Caused an infection in my eye, the doctors think my sight may be affected, which is the worst thing."

I looked more carefully now. I could not see his actual eye as it was covered with the eye patch but running down his face and nose were three deep gouges, all looking very red, angry and still infected. I felt sick to my stomach, but I quickly made the decision to act in a circumspect manner.

"That was bad luck," Angus said. "I hope that it heals soon and your eyesight is okay."

My thoughts were not so kind, more along the lines of, 'Hope the bastard is scarred for life and goes blind in that eye.'

"Goodbye then," Perryman said, "and don't forget Bettina, should you ever need an overdraft, a loan, to make an investment, or any kind of advice please contact me personally and we can discuss it in private in my office which is over there. My name is on the door."

"Thank you, Sir," I said. I was thinking, 'If I ever have to go into that office with him, I'll make sure that I have one of Vera's very long hat pins with me.'

As we left the bank, we passed his office which indeed did have a notice on the door which read:

Ernest Perryman
Bank Manager.

How I would have enjoyed changing the words Bank Manager for something which would have told the world what he was capable of! The injustice made me angry, but I dared not show it.

When I returned to Iona House, I opened my other letter which was from my old school friend Ada Smith, with whom I had been corresponding since our chance meeting at the Christmas market last year. Her letter read:

Rookey Farm
Burside.

19th October 1932.

Dear Bettina,

Dad was saying we are booked for your Christmas market again this year. He said to ask, do you want to

183

order a bird? Please let me know soon as we have taken a lot of orders already.

Still no sign of Herbert Flitch, he seems to have disappeared off the face of the earth.

Mrs Flitch has a boyfriend, which I know is hard to believe. He works at the army camp and tells everyone he's a war hero for the sympathy and the free pints. I happen to know he never went near the war, as he worked with my uncle in the munitions' factory for the full duration.

He must be desperate if he's walking out with Mrs Flitch and it is very annoying to think that he is passing himself off as a war hero. Rumour has it that they have had sex, but she always keeps her corsets and drawers on, but he takes off his truss. It's only a rumour, I don't have any proof so do not say anything.

Maisie and Fred got married and they already have a baby. Now he's gone back to sea.

Please let me know ASAP if you want a goose or something else this year.

Love,
Ada.

It was always good to hear news of the village and I wondered, having read Ada's letter, if Mrs Flitch's boyfriend was aware that she had a husband.

Stan bought the ex-Huntley and Palmer's van, smartened it up and had a proper sign writer paint on the sides:

Stanley Handyside
Gardener and Tree Specialist
Telephone 83792 after 6pm.

He had also bought a ledger as I had agreed to keep an account of all his spending on the business as well as the income. I told him quite firmly that he must get a receipt for every business purchase made, even the smallest item, for me to record. I would keep all such receipts in a box file and keep the accounts in the ledger. Stan also had invoices and business cards printed and a telephone installed at the Handyside residence as he realised that this would be an essential piece of equipment for a successful business. Both Mr and Mrs Handyside were proud of their son and they referred to him as an entrepreneur. Both parents always carried Stan's business cards with them, just in case they met a prospective client.

One Sunday Stan and I took the boys to Mallard Hall, which was on the outskirts of Ransington and where most of the new house building was. We posted leaflets through letterboxes and we even left some with the watchman warming his hands on his brazier outside the site office. I pointed out to Stan, Dora and Ian's huge 'mock-Tudor' house but I did not feel that I wanted to open the enormous black metal gates and walk up the long gravel drive with its turning circle to put a leaflet in the door.

When the leafleting was finished we took the boys to the café and bought ice creams as a treat to thank them for helping.

"Shall I get a receipt for the ice creams?" Stan joked.

"Cheeky beggar," I replied, playfully whacking him with my glove.

The boys were laughing, they loved seeing us joke together.

Ice cream licking is a serious business for a five and an eight-year-old but they still managed to talk about football. In a couple of weeks Huddersfield were coming to play our home team and the boys wanted to go to the match and Stan had offered to take them.

They had been pestering me for weeks, especially on match days when we could hear the roar of the crowd at Iona House, when a goal was scored. The football ground was within walking distance and the fans passed the house on their way home, either jubilant or disheartened, depending on the result.

"We will be so good for Stan," John said.

"I know," I said, "but Alfie is only five."

"I'm actually five and a half and I'll be six on my next birthday and I promise to hold Stan's hand," Alfie said.

Stan then said, "How's this for an idea? If my dad comes with us will you agree Bettina. We could look after a boy each — I hope you will agree."

I nodded reluctantly.

"Is that a yes then?" the three of them questioned.

"Okay it's a yes," I said.

'Just in time to knit two red and white Pom, Pom hats,' I thought.

There were shouts of delight until I added in a firm voice, "The match is nearly three weeks away, so best behaviour boys between now and then."

The boys spent the rest of the afternoon in the park kicking the ball about with some local boys. It heartened me to think that they had some friends who lived nearby.

As the day of my cheque clearance grew nearer, I began to think about the prospect of buying a sewing machine. I had read in an advertisement that a representative from the sewing machine company would, without obligation, come to the house by appointment and give a demonstration.

With Vera's permission I telephoned the number in the advertisement and arranged for a demonstration the following week. I was so excited at the prospect of owning my own sewing machine, that I just knew, I would have trouble sleeping between now and then.

I wrote a thank you letter to Great Aunt Eliza Jane and told her about the prospective sewing machine demonstration and how excited I was, experiencing butterflies at the very thought of it. I also thanked her for the information regarding Herbert Flitch who still had not made any contact with his boys in almost a year.

CHAPTER 19

The demonstration

The appointed day eventually arrived, and I opened the front door to Mr Lucas, the sewing machine manufacturing representative, carrying a sewing machine, encased in a smart wooden box with a handle.

He carefully set the electrically powered machine on the kitchen table, plugged it in and proceeded with the demonstration, consisting mostly of stitching small pieces of fabric and explaining about the correct needles to use. He encouraged me to try the machine for myself, which I did, and I found the whole experience wonderful. The electric sewing machine was so much easier for me to use, compared with the old treadle.

The agreement between Mr Lucas and I was that he would leave the sewing machine with me at Iona House for ten days on what he called 'approval'. At the end of that period he would call again and either take the machine away if I did not want it or change it for an identical new one, which I would purchase from him. However, he had not been aware, until now, that I was only sixteen, so he would require the signature of an adult. Vera was breastfeeding Rory upstairs, but he said that he was happy to wait until she came down, so I offered Mr Lucas a cup of tea which he readily accepted.

Mr Handyside called into the kitchen with some vegetables from the garden and both men chatted for a while, mostly about the weather and football. I did notice that Mr Handyside gave one of Stan's business cards to Mr Lucas.

Vera signed the necessary forms and I now had ten whole days to test and to enjoy the sewing machine. It concerned me that if it was left in the kitchen the boys might play with it, so I took it to the safety of my bedroom. I had already bought three yards of pretty yellow flowered fabric at an end of season sale, in readiness, and a summer dress pattern from Woolworths. I realised that it was now the end of October, but I had high hopes of making a summer frock ready for next year.

Mrs Handyside was very anxious for Stan to succeed in his business and one day she said, "An office is what you and Stan need Bettina, a proper office so that all the business papers can be kept in one place. Not that I want to interfere or anything."

Personally, I thought that the business was still in its infancy and a ledger and a box file seemed about right for now. However, it was understandable that a mother might be ambitious for her son, so I tried to be patient with her.

189

"Why don't you ask Mrs McLeod if you could use the tower room?" she said, obviously intent on her mission.

"Tower room? What tower room?" I replied.

Iona House had been built in the Gothic style and I had seen from the outside that it had an imposing tower, but was not aware that there was a room up there.

"Come on, I'll show you," Mrs Handyside said, excitedly.

The tower was accessed via a door, which was always kept locked, and it opened out on the side of the house into the garden. Mrs Handyside had the key and I had always been under the impression that this was an area where she kept all the household implements and cleaning materials. She unlocked the door and we entered a small entrance hall where I could see the vacuum cleaner, polishes, brass and silver cleaner, dusters, mops and buckets all neatly stored ready for use. I followed Mrs Handyside up a narrow winding staircase, and we climbed into what was the tower room.

This circular room had windows all around, giving it a three-hundred-and-sixty-degree view of the town. I could see church spires, the town hall and even as far as the river and the docks.

"What a beautiful room, has it ever been used for anything other than storage and looking at the view?" I asked.

Mrs Handyside replied, "Well, I have heard that a previous owner of this house used it as a love nest for his mistress and he had biscuit tins of sovereigns hidden in the cupboards, but I don't know how right that is."

I could see the romance of having a love nest in the sky but the possibility I had in mind for this fantastic space was a sewing room, but I did not voice my thoughts.

I went along with Mrs Handyside's idea of an office and said, "You are right, it would make a perfect office, I could keep the books straight, and sort out the invoices and Stan's work schedule in peace and quiet."

"I just knew you'd like the tower room," she said, with excitement in her voice. "I'll go and ask Mrs McLeod straight away if you can use it, if she agrees then all the place needs is a good bottoming. I'll get Percy and Mr Handyside to bring up a desk I've spotted in the cellar, along with a couple of chairs and you'll be all set."

She then went down the tower stairs, singing 'Onward Christian Soldiers', to find Vera, and seek her permission for the room to be used as an office.

I stayed back for a while looking out at the view and feeling very positive in the knowledge that this room would become my perfect sewing room.

Later that week I received a letter with a Huddersfield postmark which I thought might be from Evaleen, but it was from her mother.

56 Shapher St,
Huddersfield.
30th October 1932.

Dear Bettina,

I am writing to thank you for your kindness to my daughter Evaleen. Please would you also thank your young man Stanley. You were both very kind, bringing Evaleen home and, I doubt I can ever repay you.

You will be pleased, I know, that Evaleen has told me and John <u>everything</u>. We are a very close family and John has been very angry and upset about what happened to his sister.

It will not surprise you to know that Evaleen no longer wants to be a nanny and that she has been very lucky to obtain a position in retail. Her new job is in a lady's millinery shop which I think will suit her well. She asks me to tell you that she will write to you herself soon and to say that she is very pleased and relieved not to be in the family way.

Thank you again.

Yours sincerely,

Margaret Surtees.

PS. John says that he might be up your way for some football match, which is in a week or two.

I thought it was courteous of Evaleen's mother to write and let us know that all was well, but I was surprised to hear that her son, John, might come to the football match as I thought he was more of a rugby man.

Mrs Handyside tackled the cleaning of the tower room with a frenzy. The windows sparkled and the chintz curtains were laundered by Mrs Scribbins then rehung. Percy had already whitewashed the ceiling and walls, then the floor was scrubbed. The tower room now looked and smelt fresh and clean, if rather bare.

Unfortunately, the desk was too large for Percy and Mr Handyside to carry up the narrow, winding staircase so two tables were found in the cellar and brought up instead, along with two chairs, a rug and a small sofa, completing the furnishing of the tower room. Of course, Mrs Handyside polished the furniture to within an inch of its life with Mansion polish, which she swore by, and that, I had to agree, had an appealing smell.

I moved in the ledger and box file and stored the business cards and other paperwork in the table drawers, all the time thinking that some pretty cushions on the window seats and maybe a fresh vase of flowers would make the room perfect.

Stan, accompanied by his mother whose face glowed with pride, came up to the tower room to inspect the new office and I could see that he was impressed.

"This could be the start of your empire," she said. "Start of your empire," I heard her repeating as she went down the staircase, humming to herself.

"I like the sound of that, it would be fantastic if she is right," Stan said.

He put his arms around me, we kissed, and held each other close, he then fondled my breasts through my blouse.

'Office — sewing room — love nest, which is it to be,' I thought.

Out of respect for Stan's mother I thought it diplomatic not to take my sewing machine up to the tower room straight away. That could be a future decision which I could look forward to.

By the time Mr Lucas returned to collect the loaned sewing machine and to see if I wished to purchase a new one, my yellow frock was finished, and it had turned out well. I knew that next summer I would enjoy wearing it with its crossover bodice and short sleeves and with the leftover fabric I planned to make a dress for Claudette.

I had been to the bank and withdrawn the correct amount of cash which I handed over to Mr Lucas who in return gave me a receipt and a brand-new electric sewing machine of my very own. I could not remember ever feeling such excitement and anticipation as I did in that moment.

The endless possibilities for stitching all manner of lovely things stretched ahead of me. In the meantime, however, I needed to finish knitting the Pom, Pom hats for the boys' big football match outing.

"Dr Salmanowicz called round to see me earlier," Vera said.

I immediately felt anxious wondering who was ill.

"Don't worry there's nothing wrong. He spent some time with Rory and Claudette, and declared them both to be in good health and progressing as they should be. What he really came round here for, was to ask if we would like to have a mother's help," Vera said.

Unsure quite what a mother's help was I said, "I think I like the sound of that, tell me more."

"Well Dr Salmanowicz knows of a girl who is sixteen years old and her ambition is to become a nurse. Her name is Martha Whiley and she hopes to begin her nurse training when she is eighteen. In the meantime, she is looking for a job and Dr Salmanowicz thinks she would be perfect as a mother's help. I told him I would ask you what you think, and I will, of course, need to speak to Angus."

"What kind of things would she help with?" I asked.

"She would be expected to help with caring for Claudette and Rory mainly, but perhaps she could become involved in a few household duties and some cooking," Vera said.

"What would I do?" I said. Thinking that the things Vera was describing was more or less what I was doing every day.

"This could be perfect for you Bettina," Vera went on. "You will be helping Stan in the office and I know that you want to do more sewing."

"I suppose so," I said, feeling a little unsure.

"I think you will feel better if we actually meet our prospective mother's help," Vera said. "I propose to invite her here for an informal interview with us both. How does that sound to you?"

I knew that Vera was right, so I said, "That's a good idea, let me know when she is coming for her interview."

I'd never had an interview, let alone interviewed anyone else but I had confidence that Vera knew what to do. As for me, well, I'd just have to wing it.

CHAPTER 20

Dora

John and Alfie had made me a lovely big birthday card. Thinking that I liked football as much as they did, John had drawn a picture of a footballer on the front and Alfie had coloured it in and written seventeen in his best writing.

I was feeling happy as Stan was taking me to the pictures to see Maurice Chevalier and Janette MacDonald in 'Love me Tonight' later and Vera had suggested a birthday tea when the boys came home from school.

We had made the appointment for Martha to come for her informal interview, which was to be held in the morning room, at eleven a.m. She arrived promptly, which I took to be a good sign, and although she seemed a little nervous, she answered all Vera's questions well. A salary was agreed, along with her hours of work, which were to be Monday to Friday eight a.m. to three p.m. Martha had brought a letter of good character from her school and a reference from Dr Salmanowicz.

We introduced Martha to Claudette and Rory, and she told us that she had two younger brothers and one younger sister, so was quite used to small children. It was agreed that she would begin working at Iona House the following week.

In the afternoon, the door chimes rang, and I opened the door to Dora.

"Can't stay long Bettina," she said as she walked in. "I'm just on my way to my Women's League of Health and Beauty meeting then to Monsieur Claude to have my hair and nails done."

Dora took a great deal of pride in her appearance and she was considered to be the epitome of chic. As always, she looked immaculate in her navy-blue crepe de chine day dress and pink hat which had a bow matching the dress. Her bolero jacket was of a deep pink which suited her colouring perfectly.

"I've brought you a birthday gift which will both amaze and delight you," she said. "You will not believe it but I made it myself from instructions in a magazine."

She was almost jumping up and down with excitement, so I opened it.

The gift looked like a doll, but in fact it was a cotton dish mop on a wooden stick around which was tied a yellow duster representing the body and the face then a tea towel had been fashioned around that to look like a dress.

"Isn't it clever?" Dora said, "As soon as I saw it, I thought of you Bettina."

Words failed me for a moment and then all I could think of saying was a feeble, "Thank you Dora."

"What I was wondering," she said, "would you be a perfect poppet and do some mending for me?"

Regrettably I heard myself say, "Yes."

"Good," she replied as she ran out to her car where the chauffeur handed her the bag of things for me to mend.

As she gave me the bag, she air kissed me on both cheeks and then she said, "Thank you darling, must fly. No hurry for the mending."

"What a bloody cheek," a voice said from the kitchen doorway.

It was Mrs Handyside who had witnessed the whole charade. We decided a cuppa was needed and as we sat at the kitchen table Mrs Handyside told me that she had known Dora and her sister since they were schoolgirls, although Dora rarely acknowledged this.

"When they were young," Mrs Handyside said, "they lived with their parents quite near me and I used to see them as they passed my window on their way to school.

"Their father was an alcoholic and a gambler and because of that, he lost his job as a science teacher, which was a shame as I'm told he was a very clever man. The house had to go, and the family were out on the street.

For a while they lived in the slums in a damp flea ridden room but luckily Dora's uncle, on her mother's side, is a Freemason, so her mother, Dora and her sister were soon rehoused."

"What happened to Dora's father?" I asked.

"Died in the gutter, he literally died in the gutter," she replied. "The police found him."

"Looking at Dora and her family now, that is really hard to believe," I said.

"I know it is," Mrs Handyside said, "Dear Dora is not as posh as she'd like you to think she is. I have to say though she's always been a very smart looking girl, as is her sister."

"Dora got a job typing at the town hall when she left school." Mrs Handyside went on, "We used to see her going to work, always done up to the nines she was. Then she got a job at the law courts, as a secretary I think, and that's where she met Ian. Once she got her claws into him there was no escape, she made sure of that. Mind you, it seems that he fell for her hook line and sinker and when they were first married, they lived just around the corner from here. Very nice house it was, she had it pulled to bits, we used to joke, she's changed everything but the tiles on the roof.

"Their boys were born in that house and Vera and Angus helped them out loads, in fact I think that those boys, when they were little, lived here more than they lived in their own house. Dora likes to take Ian away for weekend breaks on their own without the children and she also liked to have them looked after while she went to the beauty parlour. Both are at boarding school now and Dora, high, mighty and full of herself, is in her big fancy house out at Mallard Hall."

I was beginning to have the impression that Mrs Handyside was not a big fan of Dora.

"As for that so-called gift, she brought you," Mrs Handyside continued, "I'd like to bet a pound to a penny that she didn't make it at all. She'll have bought it at some charity sale, she 'graced with her presence'."

To change the subject, I said, "Stan is taking me to the pictures tonight to see 'Love Me Tonight'."

My strategy worked, if there was one thing Mrs Handyside never tired of it was talking about her Stanley.

Saturday was the day of the big match. John and Alfie were excited, and I thought how lovely it would be to have Saturday afternoon to myself, just me and my sewing machine. The hexagons now joined together were big enough for a bed quilt, so I had removed the 'papers' which I found to be a rather fiddly job. Vera had given me an old blanket which I planned to sandwich between the hexagon top and the backing made from pieces of fabric which I'd joined together with my sewing machine.

John and Alfie looked very cute in their red and white pom, pom hats and they promised me that they would be very good for Stan and his dad.

Stan said, "The town is full of blue and white today, noisy Huddersfield supporters. The pubs are doing a roaring trade."

"I hope there won't be any trouble," I said.

"Now don't you worry, just enjoy having a bit of time to yourself," Mr Handyside said.

As the four of them walked down the path, I hoped that John and Alfie would be safe in the crowd.

I did have a peaceful afternoon and enjoyed pinning out my quilt on the morning room floor, although my knees weren't so happy when I'd finished.

I heard the roar of the football crowd several times and hoped that all was going well for our team. The final score was 2/2 which was a bit disappointing for us, but at least our team had not lost.

The boys said, "We had Bovril, it was great," as they ran off with their programmes, I imagined to stick them in their scrapbooks.

"Hey! Just come back here you two," I called, and they did. "What do you say to Mr Handyside and Stan for taking you to the football match?" I said to them.

"Thank you," they both said, and then they ran off again.

"Shall I call round later?" Stan asked.

"That would be nice," I said. "I can show you my, not quite finished quilt, if you like."

"Or we can do a bit of work in the tower room office," he said, winking at me.

Stan was a very kind and helpful man and I liked him very much, but I was not ready yet to turn the tower room into a love nest. A kiss and a cuddle yes, but that was it, there was no way I wanted to get pregnant, not yet anyway. There was a family planning clinic in

Ransington, down a side street somewhere, giving out appointments and advice but only to married women. There was no way I wanted to have a baby out of wedlock, I'd seen too often, the problems that this could bring to a young girl.

Vera and Angus had been so good to us, giving the boys and me a home, and Stan an office, it would be unfair and ungrateful to them to bring any more children into the house.

So, I decided that if he came round that evening, I would have a serious talk with him about what was on my mind. If he expected 'hanky-panky' then he was going to be disappointed.

CHAPTER 21

Divine Retribution

It was a ferocious storm which woke me at five a.m. in the morning following the football match. Heavy rain pelting onto my bedroom window, crashing and banging outside as fences were blown down and dustbins rolling along the road.

It was still dark, so I went to switch on the light but there was no electricity. The storm had caused a power cut. I heard Angus and Vera talking, so I knocked on their bedroom door. Apparently, the storm had been raging since about three thirty a.m.

Vera had heard it when she was feeding Rory at about that time.

"Thank goodness we have an Aga," she said. "At least the kitchen will be warm, so we can boil a kettle and cook breakfast."

Angus said, "I'm sure I can hear the back-gate banging, I'll go and check."

I found some candles in the pantry and lit a couple of them in the kitchen. I thought that the most useful thing for me to do, would be to make everyone something to eat, even though it was so early.

Angus came back in from the garden and he reported that, "Sure enough the gate is hanging off its hinges. I also think we have a fence down but I'll know better when it's daylight." He then topped up the Aga with solid fuel.

At about eight thirty a.m. Stan called in.

"I just thought I'd call to see if you are all okay," he said. "I see that you have a power cut, we have one as well. One heck of a storm it was, I've passed loads of damage on my way here."

"You're an early bird," I said.

I was pleased he didn't seem to have taken umbrage at the firm talk we had had the previous evening about sex, or rather no sex.

"I've had a telephone call already this morning about a fallen tree at the church across the park," Stan said.

"There must be lots of trees down if the crashing and banging I heard last night, is anything to go by," I said.

"The storm is over now but the church roof is down. I was told on the telephone that a big Scots Pine has been uprooted and they want me to look at it today, as the builders need to start fixing the roof tomorrow to prevent any further damage," Stan said.

"But it's Sunday," I said.

Stan explained, "They say it's urgent and the man on the phone said that he quite understood I would require double rates today for a Sunday. It's all business Bettina, so I'd better go and have a look."

When Stan arrived at the church it was obvious that the Scots Pine, he estimated to be one hundred and twenty feet high, had caused significant damage. It had fallen across the roof and partially into the church itself. It did cross Stan's mind that this could be a tricky job and he wondered if he was up to it.

After looking at the tree, Stan then went to the presbytery to find someone to discuss the matter with and he found a policeman standing at the front doorway.

Following Stan's explanation as to why he was there, the policeman went inside to find someone who could speak to Stan about the fallen tree.

An agitated man came back with the policeman and introduced himself as the deacon, and explained that it was he whom Stan had spoken to earlier on the telephone. In the man's hand was a notice which he had made, to pin to the door of the church, cancelling all services until further notice.

'Stating the obvious,' Stan had thought.

The deacon became rather quiet when they both walked around the church, looking at the tree in the roof.

To make conversation Stan said, "It is a massive tree, there'll be substantial damage. It'll be a big job for me and then for the roofers."

"Yes. No, no," the agitated deacon said. "Yes, yes, no, no unfortunately it's much worse than that; you see our priest is dead."

"What! Killed by the falling tree?" Stan asked.

"No, dead in the living room of his presbytery, it's just awful. I discovered him this morning and I called the police. We are waiting for the special detectives now," the deacon said.

"Well if the tree didn't kill him then how did he die? Do you think it could have been a fall or a heart attack?" Stan asked.

"It was an awful shock for me finding him like that." The deacon continued, "He was, and still is, lying on the floor at a very funny angle. I did not touch him. I knew not to touch him. The policeman at the door made a comment when he arrived and looked at the body, something along the lines of, 'looks like a broken neck to me'."

The deacon was now in an even more agitated state and he went on to explain to Stan that when he had arrived that morning the main front door to the church was closed but unlocked, as was the back door to the presbytery.

"Anything damaged or missing?" Stan asked, feeling like a detective himself.

"No, that's the strange thing," the deacon said. "The church silver is all complete and the charity box is still in the church untouched. Nothing seems to have been disturbed in the presbytery either, so it's all a bit of a mystery. No doubt the police will get to the bottom of it."

The man was clearly upset so Stan focused on assessing the impact of the tree and discussing the proposed method of removing it from the roof, which seemed to take the deacon's mind off finding the body of the priest and he calmed down slightly. During this discussion, more police arrived, and a van came to take the body away.

"I suppose we had better check with the police to find out if I can work here today. It will be deemed a crime scene now and I expect the police will need to check the grounds," Stan said.

"Yes, that is true, we should," the deacon said, "and there is sure to be a post-mortem."

The police gave Stan permission to begin to remove the huge tree from the church roof, but said that it would have to be later in the day, following their search of the church, presbytery and the grounds. The detective told Stan that, on no account must he go into either building as the presbytery would now be cordoned off for further examination.

Stan went back to Iona House to give the news to the family, but out of earshot of John and Alfie.

"You'd better have something to eat before you start back at the church," Vera said, as she proceeded to cook Stan a full English breakfast which he ate with a hunk of bread, washed down with two mugs of tea.

"It looks as if the job will take the best part of this week," Stan said, "but today, I'll try to get the tree off the roof, so that the roofers can start tomorrow. Will it be okay Mr McLeod if I phone my dad to see if he fancies giving me a hand?"

"That's fine," Angus said. "You go ahead Stan and if you want to borrow some heavy lifting gear, I can probably arrange that for you. We have a small crane and some heavy chains along at the works if they would be of help."

"You know what! That would be just grand," Stan said. "I would be so grateful Mr McLeod. Thank you."

"Consider it done," Angus said. "You phone your dad and then I'll get straight on to the works and arrange for the crane to be taken to the church by lorry."

"Looks as if it's all systems go," I said to Vera, who was smiling.

"Angus will love helping Stan," she said. "When we first met, his job was more of a practical nature and although he is now the Managing Director at Lansdown Short, he likes nothing more than getting his hands dirty. These last few years have been a nightmare for the steel works. This past year was especially difficult. However, I'm told not to worry, and I believe him, because by the end of this year, matters will be resolved and the works will be safe."

"Whilst the men are busy, we can have a Christmas planning meeting if you want," I said to Vera.

"What a brilliant idea," she said. "Last year was lovely if rather unplanned and hectic."

"Herbert Flitch is now living with his father in Newcastle," I told Vera. "I wonder if he will attempt to contact John and Alfie to wish them a Happy Christmas."

"If he does then I will of course, as it's Christmas, welcome him to visit his boys, after all he is their father. Do they ever ask about him?" Vera asked.

"Never," I said, "but we often talk about Mam."

The boys were both in the garden so could not possibly have overheard our conversation but we both agreed that Herbert Flitch was not much of a father.

The boys came into the kitchen and said they wanted to go to the church to help Stan and Angus. We told them that it could be dangerous work lifting such a heavy tree but perhaps, later, we could all walk to the church to see if the crane had arrived and what is happening.

The Christmas planning meeting was brief due to the demands of the children, but Vera said, "This year I'm determined to light the fire in the hall on Christmas Eve and invite the carol singers in for mulled wine and mince pies. It is something that we always used to do, a bit of a tradition at Iona House I suppose."

The entrance hall at Iona House was vast with a massive stone fireplace where I had never seen a fire lit, but imagined it would be welcoming on a cold night for the carol singers.

Food was discussed.

Vera said, "I think that we might have a change from goose, what do you think about having turkey this year Bettina?"

I agreed with her and said, "I'll write to Ada and order it tomorrow."

"A ham as well, order a ham for Christmas Eve please," Vera added.

The boys had already dropped hints about a scooter for each of them from Father Christmas, so our Christmas planning meeting did not take long at all.

Later that afternoon we walked through the park, Claudette and Rory in the Silver Cross pram and the boys kicking the ball as usual. We saw the crane before we were even out of the park and as we approached the church who should be driving the crane but Angus.

"What did I tell you. He's loving it, he's in his element," Vera said, smiling.

Angus handled the crane with expertise and he supported the fallen tree with the chains whilst Stan was on the roof using his chain saw to clear the branches and to make the trunk easier to handle.

"Big job this," Mr Handyside said. "That crane is a godsend though. It's making all the difference' I don't know how we would have managed without it."

We had taken sandwiches and flasks of tea for the men and managed to persuade them to have a break. Clearly, they needed to make progress before dark, so we did not stay long, only long enough for John and Alfie each to have a turn sitting in the cab of the crane.

As we walked home back through the park, we passed the bench where I had first seen Evaleen sitting, so frightened, that Saturday morning. I could not help

211

thinking about her abhorrent experiences and now the tree caving in the church roof and the priest dead, possibly murdered.

'Could it be Divine Intervention?' I thought. I then gave myself a silent but firm talking to, along the lines of, 'Don't be so daft Bettina.'

When we arrived home, the power cut was over, and the electricity had been restored.

Angus came home after dark looking very dirty and tired.

"Best day I've had in ages," he said. "The tree is now off the roof, so Stan will be able to work at ground level, but I reckon that he'll be there for most of the week, it's a big job, good for his business. The crane is locked up and I'll arrange for it to be collected in the morning."

Stan was there for most of the week joined by the roofers. The deacon came by at regular intervals to see how things were going.

Stan asked him, "Do you want to keep any of the tree?"

"No," was the reply. "Please dispose of it."

"I will take it away," Stan said, "but I may need to have a bonfire if that is okay."

"That will be fine but keep it small and away from the church and the presbytery," was the deacon's reply.

"I will," Stan said, "and I'll make sure it's well out at night before I leave."

"Any news from the post-mortem?" Stan asked him, on what was his third day of working there.

"Oh yes, it was definitely an unlawful death. The neck of our wonderful priest was broken with pressure from a ligature and a powerful force. As you can imagine his parents are distraught. Such a caring man, we were all very proud of him, he will be greatly missed," the deacon replied. He then went on to say, "Because of the nature of his death the investigation will be ongoing so please do not cross the barrier around the presbytery. It's an awful business, a tragic business, but I have every confidence that the police will identify and arrest the perpetrator, every confidence."

The job did take most of the week, the roofers had done a temporary repair and left. At the end of each day Stan loaded his van with logs, transporting them for storage to a garage which he rented near the docks.

Almost a week after the storm Stan was alone in the grounds of the church and presbytery, clearing up the branches and sawing the last big piece of tree trunk into logs. His bonfire was small, but burning steadily when something caught Stan's eye, something blue and trapped beneath this last piece of the tree trunk. When he pulled at it, out came a blue and white scarf with a Huddersfield football club badge stitched to it.

Stan realised that this was the evidence which might help the police to identify the murderer, however he did not need to consider his next action for long. He carried the scarf over to the bonfire where he watched it burn to ash which he then raked into a zinc bucket for later disposal in the river.

CHAPTER 22

Christmas Eve 1932

Angus and I left for the Christmas Eve market at about seven thirty a.m.

"Will you be meeting your friend again this year?" he asked.

"I hope so, if that's okay with you," I replied.

'It will be really nice to talk to a girl of my own age,' I thought.

As usual the market was very busy, and Mr Smith had a turkey and a ham already packed beautifully in a box for us.

He asked Angus, "Will you be wanting two extra chickens again this year?"

Angus replied in the affirmative which meant that Mrs Handyside and Mrs Scribbins would be happy.

Ada asked her Dad if she could have her tea break and we went to his van where we sat with steaming mugs of tea and some of Vera's homemade mince pies, which added to the atmosphere of Christmas.

"Now I want to know all about your boyfriend," Ada said. "Is he good looking? Have you gone all the way?"

I assured Ada that Stan and I had not 'gone all the way' and that, yes, he was quite good looking.

We had both read an agony aunt letter in Woman and Home about petting, which read:

My boyfriend wants me to go in for heavy petting. Please could you tell me what it is. Also is there a difference between petting and heavy petting. Also, will either make me pregnant.
Signed,
anon.

Ada and I spent some time in discussion about this but we could not quite agree as to what heavy petting actually was or petting for that matter.

"I'm not keen on lads with wandering hands," Ada said.

I listened as she told me, "I was at the young farmers dance and this lad said to me, 'can I walk you home'. We'd had a couple of dances, his teeth were clean and his breath wasn't smelly so I said to him, you can if you like but you'll have a long walk, I live over Laxlet way.

"So, he said, 'Bit of a distance that, do you fancy a snog then?' As I said before his breath smelt all right, so I said okay I'll get my coat.

"We went around the back of the village hall, there were a few couples snogging, it was dark there, so it was a good spot for a snog. I leant against the wall and he's in front of me leaning in, like you do to snog. It's all going nicely when I feel his hand up my leg, under my suspender and into the top of my stocking.

"Get your freezing hand out of my stocking top, I said to him.

"'It's cold,' he says, inching his hand nearer to my knickers.

"Get your fucking hand out of my crotch, I said, which he ignored, wanting to get on with the snog I suppose.

"Now, as I said, he's leaning into me with his legs apart so I gave him a right good kneeing into his groin and I've got strong legs with riding my horse and he jumps back screaming.

"Your balls will be nicely hot and swollen in about five minutes, warm your fucking hands on them you creep, I shouted, I hope he got the message."

For some reason we both found this funny and we were laughing our heads off when Angus tapped on the van window and it was time for me to go.

Ada said, "Come over and stay with me at the farm sometime and we can go to the young farmers dance."

"I will," I said. "Goodbye Ada, have a good Christmas, I promise to write soon."

"What was all that about?" Angus said. "You were certainly having a good old laugh."

"Oh, Ada was just telling about a boy she met at the young farmers dance," I said, not adding any details.

217

Since the storm Stan had been working every day from first light until dusk with his tree work. Many trees had fallen or had become unstable and they needed to be made safe. The office work kept me busy which was all good, as it meant that money was coming into the business.

The entrance hall at Iona House looked lovely, with the Christmas tree fully decorated and the fire glowing in the grate.

Earlier that day Stan had hung some mistletoe that he'd found growing locally and he said to me, "Well we'd better test it out then."

We kissed under the mistletoe, and then we kissed some more, unaware that John and Alfie were watching us.

The first thing we knew, the boys were wolf whistling and calling, "ooo, ooo."

Stan said in a theatrical voice, not looking at them. "What I want to eat today is a little boy sandwich."

He then went into monster mode, slowly lurching and waving his arms about calling in his best monster voice, "I can smell boys and I'm hungry."

The boys ran into the garden screaming and enjoying being chased by a monster.

Mrs Handyside and Mrs Scribbins had called for their Christmas drink and they left with a chicken for each family. We asked how Mabel was keeping and Mrs Scribbins told us that her Mabel was not well at all.

"She is under the doctor at the 'ospital with 'er 'art," Mrs Scribbins said.

We all sent Mabel our good wishes, and said we hoped that she would feel better soon.

Knowing how much Vera loved Christmas, especially Christmas Eve, Angus had arranged for the Salvation Army band to play carols in the front garden, as an accompaniment to the singers who came every year.

At six p.m. precisely we heard the sound of a solo voice singing 'Once in Royal David's City' then the rest of the carol singers joined in, along with the band, Angus opened the front door and we listened for about half an hour to, what was, a personal concert for Vera of her favourite carols.

The band and the singers were then invited into the hall where sandwiches, mince pies, mulled wine and hot orange juice were served. I noticed Angus giving the conductor of the band and the leader of the choir an envelope each, in which I expect, there would be a donation.

Bedtime for the children followed and I could tell that John and Alfie were excited, both having written to Father Christmas asking for a scooter.

When they were in the bath John said, "A boy in my class says there is no such thing as Father Christmas."

"That's a strange thing to say. I wonder what made him say that?" I said.

John went on, "The boy said it's not real, it's your dad who puts the presents under the tree, so I told him, well I don't have a dad so Father Christmas must be true."

"That's right," Alfie said, "Father Christmas is definitely real."

"Well," I said. "It's important that you go to sleep straight away tonight then in the morning we shall find out, won't we."

John, Alfie and Claudette all hung up their stockings on the brass rod over the scullery range, adding another one for Rory. A mince pie and a tot of whisky was left on the hearth for Father Christmas along with a carrot for the reindeer. All three children fell asleep quickly that Christmas Eve.

Following a delicious supper of ham and jacket potatoes I suggested to Vera and Angus that they might like to relax in the drawing room whilst I cleared away the dishes. I knew that there was to be a drama broadcast on the wireless which Vera always enjoyed and Angus could put his feet up and do a crossword if he wanted to.

Vera said, "That is very kind of you Bettina. I will take you up on your offer and by the way, we must not forget to listen to the King's speech, it will be on the wireless tomorrow at three p.m. It will be the first time that a monarch has broadcast to the nation."

The dishes didn't take long so I prepared some of the vegetables ready for our meal on Christmas Day.

The play on the wireless was just finishing when I took in the cocoa for us and I found Vera alone.

"Angus has gone for a bath," she said. "I might do the same when I've had this cocoa, as tomorrow morning could be hectic to say the least."

'That could be the understatement of the year,' I thought.

Angus came downstairs in his pyjamas and dressing gown.

He said, "I suppose Father Christmas had better eat his mince pie and drink his whisky, it would be impolite not to."

I read my book and enjoyed my cocoa. Then, I thought I'd better wrap the scooters, which I'd bought with some of the money Great Aunt Eliza Jane had sent me. Then, I put them under the Christmas tree.

It must have been about nine thirty p.m., the scooters were wrapped and under the tree so I said to Angus, "I think the children will be up early in the morning so I'm going to say goodnight."

"Goodnight Bettina, sleep well," he said.

I passed Vera at the bottom of the stairs and we hugged each other and said goodnight. She had had her bath and washed her hair. I noticed how lovely she smelt, like a meadow of flowers on a summer's day. Her hair was still damp, and she looked radiant in her blue silk kimono dressing gown.

"Busy day tomorrow, I expect," she said.

I'd been reading a magazine in bed for about half an hour when I realised that I did not feel at all sleepy, which I put down to excitement. I had left my book in the drawing room and I decided to go down for it.

Knowing the layout of the house really well I did not switch on the landing light and I was just a few steps down from the top of the stairs when I noticed Vera and Angus kissing in the hall under the mistletoe and I thought how romantic they looked so I sat down on the stairs in the dark, not wanting to spoil their kiss which I thought would soon be over.

The light in the hall was dim, mostly the warm glow from the fire, but I noticed that Vera and Angus had begun to untie each other's dressing gowns which they just let fall to the floor. She unbuttoned his pyjama top and removed it, he then took off his pyjama bottoms and then he lifted Vera's nightdress over her head, all their clothing lay on the floor and they were both completely naked. Whilst all this undressing was going on, they continued to kiss under the mistletoe.

He cupped her breasts with his hands, and she caressed him, they were oblivious to anything in that moment except each other.

I sat, rooted to the spot, not daring to move in case I made a stair creak.

Then, lying together on the warm hearthrug, in front of the last of the glowing embers they kissed and caressed each other some more, breasts, neck, arms, legs, in fact I seem to recall them kissing each other everywhere. Nothing much was said but they then made love, right there with the rosy glow of the fire on their skin. I think that they whispered to each other as they moved as one, in perfect rhythm with each other, ending with a barely audible groan.

To me this was love making between two people who were truly in love with each other. They lay there for a while afterwards, Vera stroking Angus's back, they kissed again.

I was fearful to move, mortified at the thought of being discovered, sitting there on the stairs, barely breathing.

As if on cue, baby Rory started to cry, it was time for his feed.

Angus and Vera dressed quickly, and Angus said, "I'll lock up and make sure that the lights are out."

Vera said, as she went into the kitchen, "Okay Angus, I'm just going for a glass of water and then I'll feed the baby, please make sure that the fire guards are in place."

I took this opportunity to quickly and quietly run back upstairs to my room and into bed.

Christmas Day was perfect and after lunch we gathered around the wireless to listen to the King's speech at three p.m. I thought he sounded nervous and I later discovered that Rudyard Kipling had written the speech for him which, at first, I thought was cheating but with hindsight I came to the conclusion that perhaps

Kings have people to do most tasks for them and if I was royalty I would probably do the same.

John and Alfie quickly mastered their scooters and raced up and down in the park, only falling off a few times.

"Can we have cleats in boots?" they both asked me.

"Now why would you want cleats in your boots?" was my response.

"So that we can make sparks when we are scootering," was their reply.

'Obvious really.' I thought.

CHAPTER 23

New Year's Eve 1932

The kitchen at Iona House was the hub of the family and it was invariably the place where we gathered to make important decisions. Martha or Bonny as she preferred to be called, had settled well into her role of mother's help. She and Claudette enjoyed playing together, which gave Vera more time to spend with Rory. Bonny came from a family of cooks, her father owned the local bakery in town, so she had always made cakes and biscuits and sometimes she made flapjacks with John and Alfie.

Since the storm, Stan had responded to calls from householders who either had an unstable tree or one or more that had fallen. This kept him busy, but most days he popped into the office to cash up and we would update the paperwork. I made all the entries in the ledger, kept track of jobs coming in and those completed; it was also my responsibility, to take the money to the bank, which I tried to do on alternate days, always avoiding any conversation with Mr Perryman.

I invariably had a friendly chat with whichever bank teller served me, and discovered that Mr Perryman had arranged for Mrs Perryman to be committed to the Asylum and that he now had a young live-in housekeeper. He continued to have trouble with his eye and if it did not improve, he might need to have it removed and wear a glass one.

The office work seemed to fill most of my day when I would have preferred to be sewing, but Stan needed my help, so in the evenings, when the boys were in bed, I would sometimes go up into my tower room just to have time for myself. Looking out at the night sky I found beguiling, the whole town twinkled, and I could even see the lights of the tugs as the river pilots navigated the big ships up the river. My dad's war medal was also hidden behind a secret panel I'd discovered in a window seat and on some nights, I would bring it out and hold it in my hand and think about him and Louisa.

My sewing machine was now installed in the tower room and I would sometimes be stitching until midnight. I found time to make a pretty dress for Claudette from the remnant left over from my summer frock and a skirt for Vera from a lovely piece of tweed I'd bought in a sale. However, my pride and joy is my quilt which was now finished and, if I say so myself, looked pretty good to me, for a first quilt.

"I've decided to have open house again this New Year's Eve," Vera announced one morning in the kitchen. "We always used to, so it will be just like old times."

I should never be surprised by any of Vera's sudden decisions but as it was only three days until New Year's Eve, this one came somewhat out of the blue.

"We need lists," she said. "Guests, food, drink and I'm sure Mrs Handyside will be willing to work extra hours and Bonny can help with the cooking if she agrees. We will need all the guest beds made up, in case anyone wishes to stay over, and there won't be time now to send out proper invitations, but if I give you the guest list Bettina, please would you telephone everyone. The time of the New Year's Eve open house supper will be eight p.m. until twelve thirty a.m."

I did not recognise many of the names on the list but almost all said that they would be delighted to come along to the party. Dora accepted on behalf of herself, Ian and their two sons, saying that they always enjoyed a good evening at Iona House.

"We would love to stay over," she had said.

She added that they would require two bedrooms and a bathroom which would be for their exclusive use only.

Sir Simeon Styles and Lady Rachael said that they would be delighted and as they lived some distance away the offer of an overnight stay would be perfect. Dr Salmanowicz said he would love to come, and could he bring a friend; I told him that his friend would be very welcome.

I had not met many of the people on the list but some of their names sounded familiar, as most of them were well known in the town.

The old range chimney was swept by Percy in readiness for the fire to be lit in the grate to keep the mince pies warm in the side oven. Bonny seemed to be experienced in the kitchen for one so young and soon delicious pies and pastries emerged from the Aga. Mrs Handyside cleaned and polished the house until it gleamed, and Mrs Scribbins also worked extra hours to help to prepare the guest rooms. Mr Handyside had brought the most wonderful potted plants indoors from his heated greenhouse. The Victorian conservatory, which was his domain and heated, now looked and smelt wonderful with orchids and spring flowers nestling amongst the ferns.

As the whole party had to be prepared in three days, it was 'all hands to the pump' as Mrs Handyside reminded us.

At about ten thirty a.m. on New Year's Eve I answered the telephone to Dora.

"I know that you'll all be busy today and I perfectly understand if you say no, but please could I drop Seth and Edwin off a little bit early with you as I have a hair appointment?" she asked.

'Busy is the understatement of the year,' I thought.

"I'll check with Vera," I replied.

I went back to the phone and I said to Dora, "Vera says that's fine. What time will you be bringing them over?"

"In about half an hour," was her reply.

When Dora arrived with her boys, we were all having a well-earned tea break. Seth and Edwin had brought their chess set and settled down for a game almost immediately. John and Alfie left their trains and seemed fascinated with the game of chess and the company of the older boys.

Dora said, "A little bird told me that you now have an office here for Stan's business and that you are helping him?"

"Yes, that is true," I said, wondering if Ian had told her that he was a silent partner.

"I would love to see it," she said. "A tower room, how romantic."

I asked her if her boys would keep an eye on John and Alfie for me and she affirmed that they would, so I took her up to the office, emphasising that we could not be too long as there was still a lot to do.

"I know," she said, "entertaining can be so exhaustingly hectic. Personally, I find that hiring caterers is the ideal solution."

As with everyone else who had seen the tower room Dora was captivated.

"How wonderful, so romantic, just look at that view." She waxed lyrical and was lying across a window seat. "I could spend hours up here just relaxing."

229

'Not at all likely,' I thought. 'Smoking in my sewing room, I do not think so.'

"Oh, Bettina look!" she exclaimed.

So, I looked out of the window expecting to see some strange bird or an unusual sight.

"No, no, not the view, the sewing machine, you have a sewing machine," she said with excitement in her voice. She then added, "I can bring you my alterations."

"I do not do alterations," I said, in what I hoped was a firm tone.

She appeared not to have heard me as she then went on about how she was so much slimmer now since she had been attending her Ladies League of Health and Beauty fitness sessions and how many of her outfits now required altering.

I looked her straight in the eye and said, "Dora, I'm very busy helping Stan. This is really an office and I only sew up here in my spare time, so I do not do alterations."

She still had not grasped what I was saying, because she then said, "Have you ever thought about calling yourself Betty? I think, Betty Dawson, alteration hand, sounds so professional. Many of my friends would bring you work."

I did not answer.

As she was leaving for the hairdressers we were in the hall; she lit her cigarette, securing it in its mother of pearl cigarette holder. She then told me that very soon she expected to announce that Ian was to become a

230

Judge. He had had 'the nod' so it was sure to be during the coming year and there would also be another most important event, which might require my help, but for now 'mums the word', then tapped the side of her nose.

"Be good for Auntie Vera boys," she shouted to them.

She then walked down the garden path in her cream leather spool heel shoes where her chauffeur waited for her.

"Can we stay up late to see the New Year in?" John and Alfie asked.

"Oh, I'm not sure," I replied, "that would be midnight and way past your bedtime."

"Seth and Edwin are allowed," they said.

"We will be very, very good," John said.

I then said, "I might think about it, if you have a rest in bed this afternoon then you can, or else you will fall asleep before the guests even arrive."

"Hooray! She gave in!" they shouted, as they ran off to tell Seth and Edwin.

We all helped to set out the food in the dining room and there was a fire lit in every downstairs fireplace in the house and in the guest bedrooms; Iona House looked splendid.

Vera had asked us to gather beside the Christmas tree in the big hall at seven thirty p.m., as she had something to tell us. We were all there, Mr and Mrs Handyside, Mrs Scribbins, Percy, Stan, Bonny and me waiting for Vera, who we knew would want to thank us.

She made a short speech.

"I want to thank you all for pulling together and helping me to make this New Year's Eve supper party possible, I could not have done it without you. The house looks wonderful, 'scrubs up well' as they say. There will be an important announcement later tonight, but I wanted to tell all of you first. Angus has been mentioned in the New Year's honours list and he is to receive a knighthood from the King. We will be going to Buckingham Palace for him to receive it, probably in the summer. Thank you again for all your help and enjoy the party."

Ian and Angus, looking splendid in their kilts, then came into the hall and we all gave Angus three cheers.

"Where is Dora?" Ian asked.

No one knew where she was, but I guessed that she had missed the announcement deliberately and would still be in her bedroom busy doing her five-stage beauty programme which she had recommended to me. She had told me previously that she could give an absolute guarantee, if I followed her five-stage beauty programme it would be a perfect way to make my face look more interesting and aesthetically pleasing. Needless to say, apart from the fact that there was no way I could afford her five-stage beauty programme, I would not be following her advice.

Out of Ian's earshot I heard Mrs Scribbins say to Mrs Handyside, "That Dora, she'll be clarting 'er face with those fancy creams of 'ers."

"It won't make a hapeth of difference," Mrs Handyside said. "She thinks that she's a beauty but her face is as hard as nails."

To which Mrs Scribbins added, "Eyebrows as thin as 'er lips."

As the guests arrived at Iona House, they left their hats and coats in the study which had been converted into a temporary cloakroom.

"I've never seen so many furs in my life," Bonny said.

"Shall we try one on?" I said.

Everyone was busy socialising, and so we did. I tried on a beautiful arctic fox fur jacket and Bonny looked lovely in black mink. We paraded up and down the study carpet, pouting our lips and twirling, trying to look like models; each giving a commentary on how fabulous the other looked. There was a lot of giggling between us before we carefully hung the furs back on the rail and re-joined the party. I had the feeling that Bonny and I would become good friends.

I looked after the guests for a while whilst Vera went upstairs to feed Rory. Dora circulated, looking stunning, if rather overdressed for the occasion, in a gold satin evening gown in the Grecian style. As she exuberantly networked amongst the guests, she made a point of ensuring that everyone to whom she spoke, knew that Ian was a KC.

The party was fantastic, with music, skilfully played on the accordion by Mabel Scribbins.

"Never 'ad a lesson in 'er life," Mrs Scribbins said. "Came as natural to 'er."

Seth and Edwin looked after John and Alfie who were on their best behaviour, although I did think that they started to look tired after ten p.m.

Dr Salmanowicz brought a pretty young woman as his guest and introduced her to me, as Anna, who was also a doctor from Poland and who would be helping him at his practice. He seemed fond of her and I thought that she seemed perfect for him.

The dancing went on until eleven fifty p.m., when it was time for Angus to be sent out into the garden to wait for midnight. He was tall, dark and handsome, so perfect to be the first foot.

He pretended to protest saying, "It's freezing out there with all that snow, I'll catch my death."

"Here's your coat then and remember to bring coal, salt and money back with you," Vera said, handing him a small bag which contained those very items.

We were all shouting, "Hurry, hurry, get out, there's only five minutes to go."

Vera playfully pushed Angus out into the snow-covered front garden and the door was then firmly closed behind him. We stood in silence waiting and listening for the clock in the park to strike midnight, which, when it did and the chimes heralded in the New Year along with the church bells all over town we shouted together, "Happy New Year."

There was a loud knock on the door and Angus performed his duty as our first foot giving Vera the bag containing salt, coal and a silver florin.

He then said, "Happy New Year to you all and it is my duty as your first foot to kiss the hostess," which he then did.

We all made a big circle in the hall, joined crossed arms and sang Auld Lang Syne, accompanied by Mabel on her accordion, welcoming in 1933.

I looked for John and Alfie and found them in the conservatory fast asleep on one of the wicker sofas.

The guests had started to leave, so I went, and sat with them. I was soon joined by Stan and we had a quiet moment looking out over the garden. He put his arms around me, and we kissed, I did not see sparks fly or shooting stars but his kisses made me feel warm and comfortable.

Stan said, "In the movies it would start snowing now in a very romantic snowy kind of way."

I said, "It's not snowing but the moonlight is beautiful, see how it reflects on the snow. It's as good as any moon imported from Hollywood."

We sat together holding hands and looking out at the garden covered in a blanket of snow.

Then I added, "Not much gardening for you in this weather."

"Maybe not," Stan said "but think about all those logs we have to sell in 1933. Happy New Year Bettina."

"You're such a romantic," I said "Happy New Year Stan."